# The
# And A
# Lady

### Chayeem Chronicles
### Book 1

# By
# William Siems

The Magi and A Lady
Second Printing, Revised Edition September 2020
Copyright © 2018, 2020 by William Siems

First printing - December 2018

Scripture quotations from the SUV (Siems Unauthorized Version) of the Bible.

Contact the author at Chayeem10@gmail.com

Cover by Jacob Bridgman

Interior design by Alane Pearce of Pearce Professional Writing Services APearceWriting@gmail.com.

# Dedication

Interestingly enough this fantasy novel began as a simple Christmas musical. I had scratched out about five scenes and was in the middle of scene three when another character popped up. Wait a minute, this is starting to get complicated. I soon discovered I was writing another novel (I was having trouble finding someone to write the score anyway.) Still, without the faithful support of so many it would still be lying in scraps on my office floor.

Thanks again to my wife, Nancy, who was my constant inspiration and encouragement; my good friend Keith Timmer, who listened each week to a new chapter or section and was still excited at the end; my editor daughter, Angela, "Which color would you like to see a lot of this time?" and of course the center of the whole thing Jesus, the Promised One.

# Preface

While this is a work of fiction, its inspiration finds its genesis in a second century legend called the "Revelation of the Magi" (translated by Brent Landau, published in 2010 by Harper One) which indicates that the three Wise Men were actually monks of the order of Seth (Adam's third son) awaiting the re-appearance of the Star of Eden that would precede the incarnation of the Promised One. The rest of this story comes from my own fertile imagination and is purely supposition or speculative fantasy. In addition, you will notice that in my fantasy version of the Creation story, and elsewhere, I have used my own names for the characters. It fits my "Siems Fantasy Universe" better and hopefully is not too confusing. It is my purpose, as with all my fiction, that you enjoy it, be challenged by it, and be encouraged in your journey. That is one of the reasons we have included an Advent calendar at the back of the book; that your Christmas season might be even more special.

William Siems

# Table of Contents

# Prologue

Before all things someone "other" existed. Before time, before space, before there was a "there," He simply was, the only uncreated One. The plurality of His being we would later call God, but He existed before even names, before language, words, or thoughts. He simply was. He was communion, fellowship, and friendship all rolled up in Himself. He loved to share and create, and so He did. He created the heavens and the earth and everything within them. He created the elements earth, wind, fire, and water. He created the light and the dark, the land and the sea, the plants and the animals. He created stars and angels, beings of spirit and power. Finally, in His own image, he created Man. Man's name was Clay, for he had been formed from the ground, and everything was Good. Last of all, as the pinnacle, the culmination of His creative genius, He made Woman. He called her Dawn, the beginning of all things beautiful. She was a wonder to behold. He brought her to the Man, who embraced her, and suddenly everything was Very Good.

∞

In the midst of all of the plants and animals, grew a special garden called Delight. In the center of the garden grew two trees. Originally they had been twins of each other, though not identical twins. The firstborn of all creation was named Chayeem, the Tree of Life, and the other was Daath, the Tree of Knowing. An archangel, the most wonderful and powerful of them all, was over

Delight, to cover it with his beauty and power. His name was Halel and he conducted, choreographed worship; and his light and music permeated every fiber of Delight. Then God placed Clay and Dawn in the garden as caretakers, to cultivate and tend the plants, to shepherd and protect the animals, and to assure that the "very good" of all of it grew, expanded, and flourished out into the world at large. But this assignment offended Halel. He had thought that the garden belonged to him. What right did God have to give it into the keeping of man and woman? Halel's light darkened, his music distorted. He fell from his exalted position over Delight and came to rest in the single Tree called Daath. There Dawn found him one day, perched in its branches as she foraged for breakfast for herself and Clay. Halel, sang and Dawn gasped in awe at his words, struck speechless by his voice.

❧

"May I suggest you add one of the fruit from my tree to your morning's discoveries?" he sang.

With difficulty Dawn found her breath and finally murmured, "God has said we must not eat of this tree. To even touch Daath will cause death, the loss of all things good in the world."

Halel laughed and it pierced Dawn's heart with an emotion foreign to all that she had ever known. His discordant song continued, "You will not die, God keeps this from you because He treasures it for Himself. Eating from Daath will bring a knowledge only He and I possess." Halel plucked a fruit from one of Daath's branches, drew his sword, and sliced a piece from it. He held it out to her, "Take it, there is no danger, only the enlightenment He is withholding from you."

Looking at it enticed her indeed. In all of Delight she had seen nothing like it, nothing even close. Finally, she hesitantly took it and nothing happened at all, except its juices dripped down her hand. She put it in her basket and licked her fingers. Suddenly everything the angel had said made perfect sense. God had withheld this wonder from her. She picked it back out of the basket and took a large bite of it. The pleasure of it almost unhinged her. Her surroundings looked different. Every color clearer, extravagantly filled with an alien beauty, yet also strangely unfocused all at the same time. She noticed Clay now standing at her side and she offered the rest of the slice to him. "Clay taste this! It is amazing!" She too now sang, slightly off key, rather than simply spoke the words.

∽

Clay looked at the slice of fruit, its pungent aroma surrounding him, its juices dripping from her fingers. "What is it? He questioned.

She looked at the Tree of Knowing, "A wonder we have been denied!"

"But God said," he began, but she cut him off.

"Do I look dead? I am more alive right now because of this fruit than I have ever been." She nearly pled.

Yet something did not ring true. He felt a sudden and widening distance between the two of them. He was about to lose her, lose her to this angel. In an act of desperation he grabbed the slice, ate, and they were reunited. But their union seemed tarnished. He looked at Dawn, at himself, at the angel. They were all naked and for the first time in his life he felt shame. More than feeling that he had done something wrong, something God had asked him not to do, now he himself felt wrong. He felt ashamed at himself. He had been the image of God, yet somehow he had diminished, become incomplete. He no longer measured up. He grabbed Dawn's hand and dragged her away from the tree, away from the angel. They stumbled past Chayeem to a fig tree, stripped a few leaves from it and wove them into aprons to cover their nakedness to somehow make things right again. He had to try, at least he had to try, but to no avail.

# Chapter 1
# The Promise

So many years had elapsed since the day they began to know good and evil, the day they ate of the fruit of Daath. They did not die immediately and completely as they thought they would, but everything changed and the world was no longer Very Good. Evil had secured a foothold. They knew it, experienced it, and the death they felt was more subtle. It began with a drastic alteration to their relationship with God. Before they had eaten the fruit, they had been connected, intimate, and friends with God. Now they felt distant, alienated, more akin to the enemy of them all, the darkened angel. Hal (Halel) had been cursed, felled from the tree to slither out of the garden, eating dust. They too had been cursed, Dawn with pain and the loss of her equality with man. Clay had lost the cooperation of the animals and the plants, and now experienced toil with little reward for his labor. They were summarily expelled from the garden with its wonder, awe, and beauty, and from access to the great tree Chayeem and His fruit. They wandered eastward and tried to build their own garden, but with little success. There was however, the promise. One day, the woman would give birth to a man and he would make all things new again. He would restore peace and harmony to the heavens and the earth.

Dawn, through great pain and travail, forged out of the furnace of her womb's affliction a child. When she delivered him, she called him "Kel" which means tool or weapon in hopes that he would become the weapon that would bring down their enemy, the dark angel. She conceived again and this time there was almost a sweetness to the pain. She delivered another son and he was like a breath of fresh air, a gentle breeze on an arid afternoon. They called him "Sigh." He grew up pure, spotless, and pleasing to God. Where Kel followed after his father to labor against the soil, trying desperately to bring it back into submission, Sigh became a shepherd, a friend to all of the animals.

⊙∾

One day, as he sat in the shade of a small tree beside the great river that flowed out of Delight. He had his arm around one of his sheep, Seh, as the sheep told Sigh the story of the angel's betrayal.

"After the angel had deceived your mother into eating of the tree of Knowing and your father had joined her, although he was not deceived, they left the tree and hid themselves because they were ashamed." said Seh the sheep.

Sigh replied, "Of what were they ashamed?"

Seh continued, "Of what they had become and of what they no longer were, but God did not abide their hiding. He called them out and to account for their actions. Ashamed of their nakedness, they had covered themselves with leaves from the fig tree that stood near Chayeem. However, God stripped them of their foolishness and asked for someone else to cover their shame. They could not 'take' a covering, it must be a sacrifice, freely given. So my wife, Rachel, and I volunteered to give our lives for your father and mother. We were slain and our skins used to cover their nakedness and shame. While the law says that the soul that sins must die, a greater law says that, another, a sinless one, may die in their place, so we did."

Sigh questioned, "But you are alive?"

Seh looked off in the distance, "Yes, a sacrificial death is a different kind of death, less permanent perhaps. After your mother and father left Delight, after the Tree Daath was removed from the garden, we were given new bodies. The garden was given a new gardener, and a new angel was assigned to....not to overshadow it, but to over-brighten it, if that's a word."

Sigh spoke slowly, "My father has shared some of this, but hesitantly. I think he is still saddened by what he allowed to happen."

Seh broke in, "And rightly so, but has he shared with you the promise? A child will be born who will set all things right, make all things new. Some think that you might be this promised one."

Patting the sheep fondly, Sigh shook his head. "No Seh, I am just a simple shepherd. I am nothing special."

Seh countered, "But maybe that's just it!" he exclaimed. "The dark angel fell because he thought he was more special than everyone and everything else. Maybe the promised one will think just the opposite! Besides, all your sheep think you are special." He nuzzled close to Sigh.

Sigh laughed, "Yes, yes. Like the Tree used to tell my father, 'You know, Clay, I am very very fond of you.'"

"Yes, that is what I was going to say." Seh joined him in the laughter, then suddenly his tone turned more somber. "Sigh, you know your father is planning a celebration of the promise's giving?"

"Yes," Sigh responded, "he's planning it for this next Sabbath. I was wondering what I could offer to God in thankfulness for His promise. It must be something very special."

Seh looked deeply into Sigh's eyes, "I know how much you love my first-born son, Jeruel. What if we gave him as an offering to the Lord?"

"I'm not sure what you mean?" Sigh's hand on Seh's neck stopped in mid-stroke.

Seh spoke slowly and deliberately, "Rachel and I gave our lives to cover your parents' sin. When you and your brother were born, they divided their skins to cover you, but if anyone else is born....well, they are running out of skin. Jeruel would be offered so that his skin might cover those who will be born next."

Shock brought Sigh to his feet. "What! Kill him, kill your son?"

A tear glistened Seh's eyes, "No, not kill, sacrifice. I have talked to him. He is willing to lay down his life for your future children."

Sigh was still having difficulty believing what he was hearing, but Jeruel now stood at his father's side.

Jeruel spoke, almost in a whisper, but with so much compassion that the very atmosphere reverberated with his words. "The willing gift of my life would not be a death, but a sacrifice, an offering of our best, your best, my father's best, my best. I believe it would touch the heart of God and truly show Him how grateful we are for His promise. I think it would be.... fitting and provide covering for the future."

Tears replaced Sigh's incredulity, "How would we do this? Would I have to slay you? I don't think I could do that!"

Jeruel nodded, "That is why it is called a sacrifice. It is difficult. Every part of it will be difficult."

Sigh looked up through his tears, "How can I explain this to my father? What do I tell my Father?"

Jeruel responded, "Tell him nothing. It will be a surprise, our surprise." Seh slowly nodded and they all agreed.

∽

Late that Sabbath afternoon they all gathered in the clearing that formed the center to their meager garden. Clay, Kel, and Sigh had each built a small stone altar in front of the single tree that graced their small clearing. The tree was not Chayeem, but reminded them of Chayeem. Some of their animal friends also joined them, especially many of Sigh's sheep.

Clay began, "We are gathered this evening to commemorate the giving of God's promise to one day provide a man who will set all things right, who will restore all things to being Very Good. In thankfulness to God's promise," he laid on top of his altar a small piece of leather, which he had removed from his own garment, "I dedicate these four stones which I have found in the great river that flows out of Delight; a pink Zircon for Dawn, a Diamond for myself, an Onyx for Kel, and a blood red Ruby for Sigh." He stepped back from his altar.

Kel stepped up to his altar carrying a large leaf which contained some of the produce from his garden, "I give some of the produce from my garden." He lay it on his altar and stepped back from it.

Sigh stepped forward and the first-born of his flock, Jeruel, stepped with him. Sigh's voice was choked with emotion, but increased in volume and stability as he spoke to all who were assembled. "You know the story that precedes the giving of the promise: how our parents disobeyed God, were cursed, and driven from Delight. However, before they left, their shame and nakedness was covered in the animal skins they still wear today. The skins are smaller now because they have given a part of them to cover my brother and I, but what about the future. How will we cover those born in the future. To that purpose, Jeruel willingly gives his life."

A stillness enveloped them as Sigh lay his hand on Jeruel's head. A knife appeared in Sigh's hands and he slit Jeruel's throat. Clay and Dawn gasped as blood covered Sigh and he proceeded to skin Jeruel. He then lay the naked carcass on his altar and reverently placed the skin beside it.

Accompanied by dazzling light, a huge man towered over Sigh's altar and pulled out a sword that sang with such beauty the awed assembly gasped. The being spoke in harmony with the sword's song. "I am Uriel, the angel who now covers the garden Delight. I have come for two purposes. First," he lay his sword on the carcass of Jeruel and fire fell from heaven, devouring the body of the lamb, licking up all of the blood, even engulfing Sigh for a moment, consuming the animal blood on him. The skin Sigh had removed from Jeruel, remained in the flames. Uriel continued, "Sigh, you may remove the skin from the flames." While the fire had consumed his offering, he was unharmed as he reached in and retrieved the skin, now tanned to perfection.

Uriel continued, "God is pleased with and accepts your offering, Sigh. His consuming it with fire confirms that. Second, I add to God's promise concerning the one who is to come: I, myself, will leave my covering of the garden Delight once again to herald the advent of the Promised One. I will also lead some people to meet him, to worship him, and to adore him." With that, he sheathed his sword and disappeared, leaving a final chord of music ringing in the air and a lingering fragrance of holiness.

∽

Kel stumbled away from what had begun as a celebration and ended as what? His thoughts demanded to be heard,

*"What did God mean by that?"* He felt shaken to the very core of his being. Fire and blood images were firmly emblazoned upon his mind. The fire of God had fallen from the heavens to accept his brother's offering, while exactly nothing happened to show God accepted his or his father's offering. Did not his father's offering symbolically represent the giving of their entire family to God in response to what He had promised? Maybe it had not cost his father enough, just a few hours wading in the river and some lucky observation in finding the stones. But Kel, his offering had been the fruit of his hands, the result of the sweat of his brow, and his skillful labor. To be honest he had not sought out the best of his produce. No, he had just randomly selected the items from that which the land had yielded. Sigh, on the other hand, had definitely given his best. Jeruel was the first lamb born to his flock and he had loved him like a son. To slay him before the Lord and to skin him in order to provide covering for their future children? Kel stopped in his tracks. The image of the blood dripping from Sigh's hands haunted him and caused his anger to boil. How could God reward his murdering brother with His favor? The more he thought of the unfairness of it all, the more he fumed.

Later that evening Kel found himself back at the altars, like a tongue probing a sore tooth. Sigh's altar still smoldered. *"Who could be feeding the fire? No one!"* he thought. He looked at his sacrifice. Oddly, the fruits and vegetables of his offering had already begun to rot. Clay's stones still lay atop his altar, along with their piece of skin. Kel wrapped the stones up in the skin and placed them in his loin cloth. If God didn't value his father's offering then he would. If they were gone, perhaps his father would think the Lord had taken them too and be pleased. He then went and sat with his back to the Tree. His anger continued to smolder like Sigh's altar.

Quiet words softly appeared in his heart, "Why are you angry?"

He did not respond, but simply gritted his teeth, thinking. "*Was this an offspring of the great tree Chayeem after all?*" He continued out loud "You didn't accept my offering as you did my brother's."

The Tree responded, "Be careful of your anger. Do not let it lead you where you do not want to go. You must take control of it before it takes control of you."

He spat on the ground, "Anger is just an emotion, it can not control me." He pushed away from the Tree and left the words behind him.

All night long his thoughts and dreams were troubled with images of blood and fire as his bitterness and resentment grew. Frustrated by a nearly sleepless night, he splashed some water on his faced and left for his one place of solace, his garden. He shuffled and kicked the ground along the way, covering his sandals in dust, as he walked the pathway to it. When he finally arrived he was startled to find Sigh already there, fondling the grapes in his vineyard. He had a cluster, just picked from the vine, grasped casually in his hand, lovingly caressing them for some reason.

Kel spat out the words, "What are you doing?"

Sigh startled, shocked at the tone of his brother's voice, accidentally crushed the grapes as he turned to meet him. The deep red juices dripped like blood from his hands. "Brother?" He only got the first word out when his brother interrupted him.

Kel snarled, "You have come to gloat after yesterday's demonstration."

Sigh let the crushed cluster fall to the ground and fully face his brother, unreadable emotions crossed Kel's face.

"What right do you have coming to my garden? Wasn't it enough to upstage me with your sacrifice?" his voice was rising.

"Brother, I meant no..." As Sigh searched for words, Kel stubbed his toe on what appeared to be a fist sized rock at his feet.

Kel voice was becoming maniacal. "You've always thought you were better than me. Although Father's firstborn, you are mother's favorite!" as he stooped to grasp the black stone. It fit into his hand as if made for it.

As Kel stood, Sigh whispered, "But Brother, I never..."

Before he could finish the sentence, Kel raised his hand, and brought the stone down on Sigh's forehead. Sigh crumpled to his knees. Kel hit him on the top of his head and Sigh fell into Kel's legs. Kel hit him again and again and again until Sigh collapsed onto the ground and all Kel could hear was his own ragged breathing. He threw the stone as far away as he could, stood there gasping. As the rage subsided, he looked at his bloodied hands and the crumpled form of his brother at his feet. Revulsion for what he had done began to overcome him, and the bile rose up in his throat. He began to gag. He looked quickly to the right and the left. There was no one. *"What have I done?"* He looked again. *"What must I do?"*

A plan began to form as he grabbed Sigh by the feet and unceremoniously dragged him to the compost pile. He quickly dug a hole in the pile with his bare hands, rolled Sigh into the hole, and covered him up. He then walked back to his altar, grabbed his rotting produce and took it also to the compost pile. How fitting that his rejected sacrifice should top the grave of his slain brother, amidst the flies and the stench of death. He went back to the Tree, tore off one of its branches, took it to where he had killed his brother, and wiped the trail of blood clean with its branches. He went back to the altars, broke the branch into small pieces, and burned them on his brother's altar. He walked rapidly to the river and washed himself clean. *"There! It was done! No one would ever know what had happened,"* he thought to himself as he kept washing himself off again and again and again. *"Never, never, never!"* It seemed as though a great burden had been lifted off his shoulders. Now he would be both the firstborn and the favorite. He was mistaken.

∞

That evening Sigh did not return from tending his sheep in time for supper. That was unusual. So his mother and father began to worry. Kel said he that had not seen him all day and ate surprisingly well. Self deception is a powerful thing. After supper the three of them went back to the three altars and the Tree. Clay noticed that his piece of skin and the stones were missing.

Concerned, he spoke, "Someone has removed my four stones from my altar." He looked at Kel's altar and noticed that his offering of produce was also gone.

Kel responded slyly, looking at Clay's altar, "I noticed that," he looked back at his altar, "earlier today, when I came back here, I found my produce was beginning to rot. So I took it to the compost pile. To leave it here rotting on the altar seemed an offense to God. I also noticed that someone must be tending Sigh's altar as it was still burning, but with his disappearance I forgot to mention it."

Clay and Dawn exchanged worried glances.

Then the Tree spoke to Kel, but audible to them all. "Kel, where is Sigh your brother?" They looked at each other in awe, tinged with a little fear. To Clay and Dawn, the voice sounded just like God's.

Kel responded defensively, "How should I know? Is this my day to be watching him?"

The Tree continued, "I hear the voice of his blood crying out to me from the ground. Kel, what have you done?"

Kel collapsed trembling to his knees. He had seemingly hid nothing.

A great sadness filled the Tree's voice as a cloud suddenly blocked the sun, "The ground which has opened up to receive your brother's blood will no longer open to you. Rather you will be a fugitive and wanderer on the earth."

Kel lifted a fist towards the Tree, shaking it as he spat out the words, "Why don't You just kill me, like You did the first lambs to clothe my parents, like Sigh did his lamb, like I did my brother? I know you are a wrathful God."

The Tree responded with so much compassionate authority that tears filled the eyes of all, "You have no idea who I AM!"

"Then whoever sees me will kill me!" he stammered.

"No!" spoke the Tree. Suddenly a black mark appeared on Kel's forehead. A death mark rather than a birthmark. The Tree's words echoed, "Whoever kills Kel will share in his curses sevenfold!"

# Chapter 2
# Wandering

As the sound of the Tree's words dissipated, Kel got up and staggered away from the altars, the Tree, and from the presence of God. He had extinguished his parents' "breath of fresh air" and for that he was forever banished to wander in the lands of Agitation, without solace or comfort. But because he was the son of Clay the greatness in him, although now twisted, did not allow him to perish in the wilderness. Rather, he developed his own lifestyle, that of a vagabond.

Meanwhile, Clay and Dawn had other children, but none of them replaced the ache in their hearts left by the loss of Sigh. One child, a daughter named Hope, did grow up as a special blessing to them both. However, as a woman, she could not be the Promised One. That must be a son. That did not stop her from becoming excellent at everything she did, because the favor of the Lord was upon her. Humans and animals alike loved her.

On a particularly beautiful afternoon, as she was puttering in the garden that had once belonged to Kel, the Tree spoke to her. "Hope, I have a difficult task for you. Pack a few things and take a little food and travel East. I will show you the way."

Hope knelt in the soft garden soil in front of the Tree, "What do I tell my father and mother?"

The Tree continued, "You may tell them simply, that I will take care of you."

ᢒᢇ

Hope did as the Tree had asked of her. She packed a few things, a little food, and told her parents she was traveling to the East under the guidance and protection of the Tree. They wept, kissed her, released her into the care of the Tree, and she began to wander eastward. Her travel that first day was uneventful, although the young camel, Beker, that accompanied her thought it was a bit hot there in the desert. Perhaps they should have traveled during the night. They found an oasis shortly before dark, ate some of their food, and lay down to sleep. Hope had found enough wood to start a small fire. Lying with her head on Beker's shoulder, she took out a small harp that her father had made for her, began to play a simple melody, and then sing. Beker joined in and harmonized.

> *I sit amidst the evening stars,*
> *content with the life the Tree gives,*
> *He is (after all) the Tree of Life,*
> *Chayeem is his name.*
> *While wandering both near or far,*
> *I happily embrace what comes today,*
> *It matters not if it's good or ill,*
> *His light and love are all the same.*
>
> *He is the one I see in the sun or find*
> *in the clouds and the rain.*
> *He is the one that brings me joy,*
> *His love makes it all the same.*

Suddenly Beker flinched and startled Hope. They had not heard him approach. Just outside the circle of fire light stood a man of the desert. "I...heard...you...." He spoke with difficulty.

Hope smiled, "Greetings, friend." He said nothing more. She continued, "You need to know that I travel under the protection of the Great Tree, Chayeem!" She tried to sound authoritative. He had flinched noticeably at the Tree's name. "Do you live around here?" She asked.

"A....few....days...further to the East." He spoke as though unaccustomed to doing so.

Now as she talked she tried to sound and remain calm. "I have a brother who lives in that direction. His name is Kel. Perhaps you know him?"

He flinched again, "I....haven't...heard...that....name... in a long while. He is no longer called that, but goes by the name Halek, the wanderer."

Beker joined in, "So, you know him?"

Now the desert man was startled. Perhaps he was unused to camels speaking. "I have heard of him, there are stories."

Beker stood beside Hope and had inched a bit between her and the desert man. "What do these stories say?" he questioned.

"That he came from the West, that his parents grew up in the garden Delight that lies further to the West where man is no longer allowed." His speech was coming easier now.

Beker now completely shielded Hope, "And do these stories say why he left?"

The desert man's speech slowed again, but this time the words seemed to pain him, "Only that there...was... some trouble and he left under... a kind of... cloud."

Remembering her manners she asked, "Would you like some food, some water." He stepped somewhat into the light. There was a horse behind him, still shrouded in the darkness.

He did not quite smile, but his demeanor did relax a bit. "Yes, that would be kind of you." He now stepped fully into the firelight and removed his turban. The blackened mark stood clearly out on his forehead.

With a gasp Hope exclaimed, "You are Kel, my brother, the one now called the wanderer?" He nodded. Her heart was filled with conflicted emotions. Here was her lost brother, but also the one they said displeased God and murdered her brother. Yet she felt a measure of compassion for him.

His smile broadened a little, "Yes, please excuse the small deception." He sat, crossed his legs, obviously expecting her to serve him. Despite her apprehension she felt the Tree's nudge to do so and rose.

"And does your horse have a name?" She smiled a little at the horse.

"He is called Choom."

Now smiling broadly, "Beker, would you show Choom to the water, I will be fine here. He is after all family."

Reluctantly Beker left her side, "Choom, if you would like to follow me?" The horse and the camel journeyed to the water and drank deeply, while Hope served Kel what remained of their meal. The next morning, Hope felt the Tree's prod to join Kel in his wandering. In time, as Kel began to understand what a wonder Hope was, they became more than family, they became friends. Partly out of necessity and partly because she seemed to enjoy it so, he taught her what he had learned of woodcraft. As his heart began to heal under her touch, the mark on his forehead lessened, and one starlit evening she consented to be his wife. She eventually gave him a son, a wonderful child, but that is another story.

# Chapter 3
# The Story

Clay and Dawn had lost both of their firstborn sons and they grieved for them and the seeming loss of the promise. They grieved deeply and long and yet in the midst of their comforting, another child was conceived between them. In the fullness of time, there was born to Clay and Dawn, a son to take the place of Sigh, whom they had lost. Because he set in their hearts in the place previously occupied by Sigh, they called him "Set." Set grew up in favor with God, man, and even the favor of animals was upon him.

One day, as they sat under a tree, by the river, in the cool of the evening, Clay shared a story with his young son Set.

He said, "In the beginning, when the morning stars sang for joy and the sons of God shouted with them, one star was appointed to shine over Delight. He was special, the anointed archangel, chosen to provided the covering light, beauty, and music for the Tree of Life and all of the Garden Delight, but his exalted position became his undoing and corrupted his heart. Darkened, he led a rebellion against God Himself and was thrown down from the heavens. He dwelt in the Tree of Knowing until he fell from that position too and was banished from the garden. He had tricked your mother into eating from the Tree of Knowing against God's explicit command. I too chose to eat from it. For that we were both expelled from the garden. However, before we left, we were promised that the day would come when God would send a man, perfect like I had been, who would restore all things. Another star, an angel who was humble of heart, was assigned to cover the Tree and the Garden. This angel promised to once again appear to the world and precede the coming of the Promised One." Clay continued, "So, we need to be ever vigilant, ever watchful, for we do not know when this herald of His coming will arrive."

Set smiled as he responded, "Father, perhaps we should include a simple ceremony in our weekly Sabbath remembrance? A ceremony that remembers Delight, Chayeem, and the star that will proceed the coming of the Promised One?"

Clay was pleased with his son's reply and the next Sabbath they added the ceremony, just as Set had suggested.

# Chapter 4
# The Magi (Masters)

Sepheth- Master of Languages

The remembrance of Delight and the One Tree has been handed down from generation to generation until this very day, when the three Masters had their weekly gathering. They are meeting at Sepheth's, the Master of Languages' School. He greeted them at the door. "Gentlemen, welcome, I so look forward to our getting together each week."

Raz, the Master of Mysteries, responded, "Yes, our time together is always a highlight for me too."

And Chokma, the Master of Religions, added, "And as hard as it is for me to do....I agree, for once, with the both of you."

As they found their usual seats, Lady Hannah glided in with a smile, carrying a tray containing cups of wine and a bowl of cut up fruit.

Noticing her entrance Seph affectionately said, "Ah, Lady Hannah, the best part of any day is you, and of course that which you carry."

Laughingly, she placed the tray before the three of them, bowed slightly, and left the room.

Raz addressed Seph, "You have brought the sacred scroll?"

Frowning, Seph countered, "Of course I did. In all of our meetings, have I ever forgotten it?"

Chok chuckled, "Only too many times to remember, I am afraid."

Seph's frown softened and then turned to laughter.

More seriously, Raz spoke reverently, "Well go ahead, read from it. Although we all know what it says by heart."

⌒

Seph cleared his throat multiple times, to enhance the importance of what he was about to read. "Ahem, ahem, ahem. Since the dawn of time, the fruit of the Tree of Life...," he paused, "Have I ever told you the meaning of the name of the Tree of Life, Chayeem?"

Chok raised his eyebrows, "Yes, you have Seph, but go ahead, you seem to so enjoy repeating yourself."

Seph increased the gravity of his tone, "The literal translation is plural. So you could say it really is the tree of Lives, or breaths, or panting, or winds, or you might even say it means, Ha, ha, hahahahah, Laughter. I know it almost seems irreverent, but it is nice to know that the

God of the Universe also has a sense of humor. I guess it should be expected that He does, since He is the creator and source of humor."

Chok quickly added, "And He did, after all, create you. That most definitely proves that He has a sense of humor."

Seph scowled while the other two laughed.

Then he continued almost regally, "The fruit of the Tree of Life in the garden, was eaten by every living creature; man, animals, and angels, and it provided them all the inner life that allowed them to communicate with one another."

"As a Master of Languages you would appreciate, Seph," Raz interjected matching Seph's graveness, "that there wasn't a universal language, but that it was the Tree of Life that brought them a unified understanding, each of the other."

Seph looked intently at Raz, "And as a Master of the Mysteries, you would appreciate the mystery of that experience."

ᘓᓄ

He continued reading from the scroll, "And so, to commemorate the awe and wonder of the One Tree, we celebrate and remember the efficacy of His fruit by partaking of the fruit of our labors."

Each of them took a piece of fruit from the bowl, raised it, and said in unison, "We thank You Almighty God, King of the Universe, for responding to our labors by providing this fruit." They each ate the fruit.

Seph took the lead again as he lifted a cup. "And we, Your children, speak praise to Your great name by raising the cup and drinking of the fruit of the vine."

The other two raised their cups, took a sip, and then they all repeated in unison again. "We are thankful for Your provision of all that we need, each and every day."

They drained their cups and then placed them back down on the table.

Chok sighed as he closed his eyes, "Yes, I have always appreciated this ceremony, but now, on to other things. Seph, you mentioned that you had found an ancient manuscript."

Seph smiled mischievously, "Yes, but it's only a fragment of one, written in a language with which I was unfamiliar. It seems faintly Hebraic, but predates anything I have ever seen before. I think, however, that I have been able to piece some of it together."

Raz jumped in, "And what have you been able to piece together?"

Seph's smile broadened, "It speaks of a star or an angel, I'm not sure which the term refers to, that was present in 'the Garden of Delight, with a special relationship to the Tree of Life."

Chok's eyes were wide open now, "An angel, what does it say about this angel?

Seph continued, "It seems to say that this angel, if that's what it is, will come again and precede the coming of the Promised One, the man who brings about the release from all that is wrong in the world and restores all things to their original state of purity and beauty."

"So it is a prophecy of the return of this angel?" questioned Raz.

"So it would seem. Him or the star, I'm not sure." Seph answered.

Chok closed his eyes again. "The Religions also contain hints of such an event. It is called by different names, but in each event it focuses on the reconciliation of the relationship between God and man. It speaks of the final sacrifice that will make everything right again. It will be the coming of the king of righteousness."

Raz, matched Chok's majestic tone. "The Mysteries also point to such a momentous event. It is foreshadowed even in the eating of the fruit and the drinking of the cup that we have partaken of this evening and that we do so together each week; it foretells a return to the innocence and purity of our relationship with the One Tree, Chayeem, the Tree of Life."

Seph, commandingly regained the lead of the conversation. "So, let us join in an attitude of prayer as we sing the "Song of the One Tree", and they sang the four verses in three part harmony, joining in unison on the chorus.

> *The light was young and the garden new*
> *Before there was evil and strife*
> *In the days of old when the One Tree grew*
> *In the midst stood the Tree of Life.*

> *Chorus:*
> *Help us return to those blessed days*
> *Before there was darkness,*
> *suffering, and pain*
> *Help us return to when all things were new*
> *To stand unashamed 'neath the*
> *One Tree again.*

> *The Archangel fell from his own place of grace*
> *Because of his beauty and pride*
> *He then tempted man to turn from God's face*
> *And both disobeyed and they died.*

> *All is now fallen and under a curse*
> *Darkness has covered the land*
> *And yet there is hope for God sent a verse*
> *A promise that God will restore man.*

> *God's grace and His mercy will blossom afresh*
> *As all things become new again*

*When God takes away the reproach of our flesh*
*And pays for the debt of our sin.*

*Chorus:*
*Help us return to those blessed days*
*Before there was darkness,*
*suffering, and pain*
*Help us return to when all things were new*
*To stand unashamed 'neath the*
*One Tree again.*

As their voices held the last note of the final chorus, Hannah entered silently to refill their cups. As she turned to leave, she abruptly stopped. Something had arrested her attention. As she began to turn back around, one entire portion of the room had been flooded with light from an unknown source. A powerful voice spoke out of the light! "I am Uriel and I stand before Him, Who was, and Who is, and Who always will be."

The three men cowered in fear, but Hannah completed her turn, dropped to her knees, and in a mixture of rapture and awe, faced what appeared to be an angel.

Uriel's voice echoed throughout the room, "I have come, as commanded, to bring you good news. The One who was spoken of so long ago, the One who has been foretold, the fulfiller of all that was promised, has been born in the lands to the West, and I will bring you to Him. I am but a pale reflection of the light which He will bring to his people, Israel, and then to all mankind. Therefore, in order to guide you to Him, I have come."

As quickly as the light and the angel had appeared, like a candle snuffed out, both the light and the angel were gone.

Hannah regained her composure first, "Wow! That was pretty amazing!"

Seph, still visibly shaken said, "Is that what it's supposed to feel like when prophecy is fulfilled? Like you just got punched in the gut?"

Raz's voice was beginning to turn into Hannah's awe as he said, "I'm not sure I have ever been present at the fulfillment of prophecy, so I'm not sure what it's supposed to feel like, but the angel of God speaking to us..." He left the sentence hanging.

Chok picked up where he left off, "Well, I think that awe is just supposed to be "Ah!" with an extra bit of awe thrown in for good measure." He chuckled.

Finally regaining his composure Seph added to the conversation. "This is my first encounter with an angel, but I'm a little confused. He said he was supposed to guide us to the Promised One and then he disappeared. Does that seem strange to any of the rest of you?"

Hannah threw in her opinion, "Ummm, he is an angel. I don't think he's answerable to us."

"Hannah does have a point, Seph," Raz commented.

"I know, I know, but what do we do next?" Chok almost pleaded. "Maybe we should ask Him." And he pointed upward.

He began, "Almighty Everlasting God of the Universe...."

Seph interrupted him. "I don't think you need to rehearse His entire pedigree. I think you can just talk to Him, like He's right here, because He is."

Raz said matter of factly, "God, You sent us Your angel, Uriel. What would You like us to do now, besides just wait?"

Hannah chimed in, "I'm pretty sure He just wants us to wait."

Raz asked, "Anyone else?"

Chok added, "I would agree with Hannah, just waiting makes a lot of sense."

Seph thought for a moment, then proposed. "How about if we also do some research? Like the best route we could take to Israel, since he did mention it. Also what we might need for the journey, considering the time of year and everything?"

Raz spoke, "Yup, that couldn't hurt."

Seph was back in control. "Hannah, do you want to begin looking into food and lodging along the way to Israel?"

"Sure I can do that."

Seph continued, "I will look through my Library for anything else that might help us."

"While I will consult our society of mysteries for any other possible clues..." Raz offered.

"And I will speak to my religious brothers and see if they can shed any additional light on this." offered Chok

The three Masters stood, embraced each other, and then Raz and Chok departed without their usual farewells.

# Chapter 5
# Preparations

While they began the preparations for a trip that they did not fully understand, they each did so the way they understood best. They found there was no prior evidence of an angel named Uriel in any of the ancient writings that were available. There was, however, a significant amount of evidence concerning a person called "the Promised One", that he would be the man who would bring peace to the world and an everlasting kingdom. After six days, all their planning and preparation was finally complete. They were now ready to depart at a moment's notice. The Three Masters gathered again for their weekly meeting and the ceremony of the One Tree. Having completed it. Hannah entered to replenish their drinks only to find that the angel Uriel had joined them again. This time he was not an imposing eight cubit tall being whose radiance created more fear than awe. This time he appeared as an old man, but they still recognized him.

Hannah set down the pitcher and bowls as she said, "Master Uriel, may I get you something to drink?"

The angel replied, "Thank you Hannah, that would be very nice and bring a cup for yourself." She turned to leave as he continued, "And Hannah, there is no need to call me master. I am simply a servant of the Most High like yourself."

Hannah left and returned with two cups. They had pulled a fifth chair up to the table. They all stood and Uriel motioned for her to sit in the empty chair next to him. She did and he filled both their cups.

Seph continued, "Uriel, you were saying?"

Uriel continued, "Yes, I believe that you have nearly finished all your preparations and just in time as we need to leave this evening. We will be traveling initially under the cover of darkness so as to avoid undue notice. Our mission is not particularly clandestine, but there are those who would attempt to thwart its purpose. It will pay for us to be circumspect."

Raz leaned over to whisper to Chok, "Is he always going to talk in riddles?"

Uriel responded to his whisper, "I heard that Raz."

"I'm sorry, Sir, I meant no disrespect or offense." Raz apologized.

Uriel chuckled. "Not a problem, none taken."

Seph interrupted the flow of things. "Since we are going to Israel, I assume we will be stopping in Jerusalem?"

"At this point that is probably a valid assumption." Uriel said.

Chok asked, "You are familiar with the route which we have planned out?"

Turning to him, Uriel replied, "Yes, and it is a good plan."

"And you will be going with us?" assumed Raz.

Uriel's smile faded a bit. "Yes, although you will not usually be able to see me, I will be with you. You can depend upon that." And he disappeared from view.

They looked from one to the other and Seph spoke, "His coming and goings are a little disconcerting." He visibly sighed. "What do we have left to do to be ready?"

Hannah answered first, "I believe that all we have left to do is pack up our individual supplies, load the horses, and we are ready to go."

Raz added, "Since Uriel has us traveling at night, I guess that means we will be sleeping during the day, and that we will need to be guarding our tents in shifts?"

Seph agreed. "Yes, that is probably true. Hannah, can you take the first watch each day after we set up the tents and you have bedded down the animals?"

"Yes, that should work just fine." She added. "As long as I don't have to do all of the cooking too."

Chok grumped, "I don't sleep very well during the day."

Seph shot back in return, "That's Okay, this is a mission not a vacation, deal with it." Then he laughed.

Chok still complained. "I was just saying."

Raz intervened, "We'll do fine, Chok. Just remember who we are going to see, the Promised One, and Uriel will be with us, even if we can't see him. What could possibly go wrong?"

Chok replied pessimistically, "All kinds of things could go wrong; bandits, bad weather, a variety of personal calamities..."

Seph teased, "And someone who worries like an old woman, no offense Hannah.

A smile flickered across Hannah's face. "I didn't think you were talking about me, I'm not that old." And she laughed openly.

Raz joined the laughter, "Ha, ha, ha..." And then his tone changed and became more serious, "If we are truly to meet the Promised One, wouldn't it be expected that we bring Him gifts?"

"Most certainly, gifts in accordance with His majestic stature and I'm afraid that I have nothing worthy of such a person." Chok worried.

Seph's smile widened again, "Well, you don't have much time to figure it out. We leave as soon as we are packed. I believe that you should simply ask Him." And he pointed upward as Chok had done earlier.

Raz smiled too, "Touche' Chokmah!"

As the others left to prepare, Hannah sang, reverently in a whisper,

> *Preparing for a mission,*
> *about which we know little*
> *and doing what is necessary,*
> *doing what we must.*
> *Not knowing where we're going makes it some*
> *what difficult,*
> *Our following the messenger should help to*
> *build our trust.*

> *Chorus:*
> *We prepare, that we might go,*
> *and he prepares the way*
> *We prepare things practical,*
> *he prepares the rest*
> *We prepare to follow him, each word that he*
> *might say*
> *In everything we are prepared and hope the*
> *rest is blest.*

> *He represents the Promised One,*
> *who's making new all things*
> *The one who brings us back to God,*
> *the one that's been of old.*
> *He leads us on to where he'll be,*
> *sometimes without his wings*
> *The angel star that shows the way,*
> *that Clay once foretold.*

*We travel incognito, we're traveling at night*
*Following an angel we usually cannot see*
*We're traveling in darkness,*
*    searching for the light*
*Hoping he will lead us to where we need to be.*

They left that night to begin their journey. Sleeping by day, the three Masters and the Lady managed the first leg of their journey without incident. Even though they were on a mission to find the Promised One, it sometimes seemed like they were on holiday. They told stories, often on one another, and related the legends of old. They also read from a copy of the ancient Hebrew Scriptures that they had brought with them, of how God had rescued His people on occasions too numerous to mention and how He had promised to do it again. This was who they were searching for, the rescuer, the redeemer, the Liberator.

# Chapter 6
# Early One Evening

While the three Masters set up the tents and unloaded what they needed from the horses, Hannah then bedded down the horses for the day, and took the first watch as the Masters slept. She often also had the last watch, as she did this early evening. They were far enough off the main road that they thought they would not be bothered by a lot of travelers and yet there were still a few that discovered them from simple curiosity. Hannah had heard one of the horses whiny. A stranger stood in the trees, watching the camp.

Because the fire was between them, he could not see her. Stealthily Hannah walked back into the deeper darkness, circled around behind him, and cleared her throat, "Ahem!"

The man turned swiftly and drew his sword in a single fluid motion. Its release from the sheath and swinging arc produced a chord of achingly sweet music.

Hannah was momentarily awestruck at the sword's song, but quickly recovered, "What do you want?"

The stranger's challenging demeanor softened measurably. "Oh, it's a woman," he said as he sheathed his sword and the music ceased.

She continued, "My question remains unanswered."

A slight smile graced the stranger's face. "I meant no harm Miss. I stumbled across your camp here, so far off the road in the early evening, and was puzzled."

It was difficult not to return his smile, but Hannah managed. "It is no great puzzle. We are Bedouin, from the desert. We are used to traveling at night when it is cooler. The rest of us will be awake shortly," she said as a caution.

He was still puzzled. "Ah, but you are no longer in the desert and yet you continue to travel at night?"

A slight smile finally began to grace Hannah's face. "Old habits die with difficulty."

"And they let you, a woman, guard their camp?" The stranger's puzzlement deepened.

So did her smile. "Sir, you do not know me. I may be more capable than I appear."

The stranger's tone became a bit sarcastic. "I doubt that, but let me introduce myself..." As he held out his hand.

She quickly grasped it in a peculiar way, and the stranger found himself on his knees in incapacitating pain. She let go of his hand and replied, "I'm sorry, you were introducing yourself?"

Shaking his hand, he slowly got to his feet, looked at his hand and then back at her. "I think I am sorrier than you." Massaging his fingers, palm, wrist, he continued, "It seems I have misjudged you."

It was her turn for sarcasm, "You and most of your gender."

"I am Mishimar." He bowed slightly. "May I inquire where you are headed," he chuckled slightly, "...at night?"

Hannah turned to the horses. "We are initially headed for Jerusalem."

A bit sheepishly he responded, "I was going to offer my services as a guard, which you obviously don't need, but

I am still wondering if I might journey with you? There is often greater safety in numbers, rather than when one is traveling alone."

"Well, I believe I speak for the rest of us that you are welcome to at least join us for our meal. Perhaps you can then explain how you came to possess one of the singing swords. Do you have a horse?" He nodded. "Then if you would like to go fetch him, I will assure the others are awake and start preparing our meal."

"Thank you," he said as he turned to go.

Before Hannah could awaken the others, she was intercepted on her way back to them by Uriel, who appeared again as an old man. "Who was that?" He pointed in the direction Mishimar had left.

"That is Mishimar, a soldier of some kind," she replied. "He would like to travel with us to Jerusalem."

"Ah." Now Uriel smiled. "I was wondering when he would finally make contact with us. He has been following us."

Hannah was surprised. "I thought you were protecting us from people like him?"

Uriel chuckled. "And I am. Being invisible does have its advantages and my senses are more acute than yours. Not being as constrained by space as you are, I have been checking him out for the past several days."

Hannah questioned, "Will it be all right to have him with us? He isn't planning to rob us or anything, is he?"

Uriel, still lightly chuckling, replied, "No, it will be fine. In fact, having him with us will be to our advantage. As you just witnessed, you do not appear to be much of a deterrent, being a woman, but having a soldier with us will make us look more formidable and provide an additional layer of safety to our journey."

Her questioning continued. "He has one of the singing swords."

"Yes, he does." Uriel replied, rather matter-of-factly.

"But where would he come by one of those?" she asked. "That's a question that you need to ask your soldier friend." And he was gone.

Without trying to appear presumptuous, Mishimar had gone back to his camp and broke it, packed up his gear, and returned with his horse, ready for travel. When Hannah returned to their tents she found Seph had rekindled their fire and had some water boiling. She quickly assembled their simple breakfast, and was serving it as the sun set, the dusk deepened, and Mishimar walked up leading a beautiful black stallion.

Hannah had shared with the three about her meeting with him and with Uriel in a cursory fashion, but one look at his horse and she knew much more about this mysterious stranger. Hannah introduced him to them, "Gentlemen, this is Mishimar, whom I just met and invited to eat with us. He would like you to consider allowing him to accompany us to Jerusalem."

Seph, Raz, and Chok were seated around their small campfire with their plates in their hands. The three of them put their dishes down, struggled to their feet, and advanced to greet him, their right hands extended. They all looked a little advanced in years, but after his experience with Hannah Mishimar approached each handshake with caution. What happened surprised him anyway.

Seph grasped his hand, gathered him into an embrace, and kissed him on both cheeks. "Hannah has told us a little about you and it seems she considers you a friend. If you are becoming a friend to her then you will also become ours."

Raz followed suit and embraced him with a smile, "It seems Uriel accepts you also and that speaks volumes on your behalf."

Mishimar pulled back and questioned, "Uriel?"

Raz continued, "He is also traveling with us, but," and he looked around, "I don't see him at the moment."

Chok's smile was a bit forced as he too embraced their new friend, "I hope you have brought your own rations."

Mishimar disengaged from Chok and looked at all four of them. "Then I may accompany you?" They all nodded, Hannah adding, "Here, let me have your horse." She reached out a hand for the reins. "Please, sit down and share our meal." Her own smile deepened as he handed her the reins and sat down with the men while she walked his horse back to where theirs were standing. Over her shoulder she called, "What's his name?"

"Zillah" he responded.

"Ah," she nearly sang as she snuggled her head into his neck and scratched him behind the ear. "Shadow, that seems appropriate for a horse traveling with us at night." Zillah nickered.

# Chapter 7
# Another Singing Sword

While Hannah was gone the three of them shared with Mishimar the basic elements of their story: That they were masters of language, religion, and mysteries. That they were keepers of the One Tree ceremony that included the return of the Promised One who would make all things new. That the return of the One would be preceded by the appearance of an angel/star who had originally covered the garden of Delight and the One Tree. That this same angel, Uriel, had appeared to them and was now leading them to Israel and the Promised One. Mishimar asked very few questions. He just nodded at appropriate times as they spoke and then, when they were finished, he finally said, "Then I am even more honored to be joining you on such a journey. Fate must have guided me to you."

Seph corrected him, "We don't believe in fate. We believe in Chayeem and if He has led you to us then we are pleased to have you join us." Mishimar nodded as Hannah joined them.

She was still a bit in awe of his horse. "That is truly a wonderful horse you have brought with you."

His smile came easily and she was beginning to think, often, "I'm not sure who brought whom. We have been together since my father gave him to me ten years ago. He was a present on my eighteenth birthday, as was the sword I carry."

Her awe deepened, "I would not have guessed him to be that old."

"I'm not sure he ages, although I am sure that I do. You see, I didn't have a chance to ask my father where the horse came from. We were just celebrating the reaching of my maturity when our home was attacked. My father and our entire family, servants and all, were destroyed. I alone escaped on the horse, with the sword."

A sudden tear graced Hannah's cheek, "I'm sorry…"

He interrupted, "Thank you, but you don't have to be. My father and family had lived full and wonderful lives and they are living even greater ones now, having joined Chayeem." He turned to Seph,. "I'm sorry for the small deception, Seph, but I don't believe in fate either. It was just my small attempt to make sure that you really knew Him and were not just followers of religion, the mysteries, and languages."

They looked at one another and nodded their understanding as he continued. "And I am sure you are wondering about my sword." They nodded again. "Legend has it that there were seven singing swords forged before the world began and that they were given to the archangels. During the rebellion of Halel, two of the swords fell with the Nephilim and one was lost when R'gel was slain."

Seph interrupted him, "That is more than mere legend. The story is corroborated in a number of ancient manuscripts. One of the strongest and most complete accounts being given in the Chronicles of the Elohim."

Mishimar looked at him more sternly then he meant to. "May I continue?"

"Yes. I am sorry I interrupted you."

"There is also a legend as to what happened to the singing sword that fell with one of the Nephilim. The former angel to whom the sword belonged had relations with a Moabite woman. A bastard son was born and was named Goliath, the exile. He was probably called that because he seemed only half human, his mother claiming that she had lain with a god. When Goliath reached his maturity and was more than six cubits tall, he fought and slew an Ariel bare-handed. The Ariels are lion-like beings that the Moabites worship. His slaying of it, especially bare-handed, confirmed his semi-divinity to the Moabites. At the celebration of this feat and his entrance into maturity, he was visited by an Angel of Indescribable Beauty and given the singing sword which had belonged to his father."

Seph could not help himself. "Goliath, the giant, had one of the original singing swords?"

"Yes," continued Mishimar. "As your ancient Hebrew scriptures record, after David knocked him unconscious with the stone from his sling, he slew him by cutting off his head."

"And what happened to the sword?" Seph was nearly beside himself with excitement.

"David took the sword and placed it in the tabernacle as a trophy to God's power and faithfulness, where it lay until he retrieved it one day while fleeing from king Saul."

Chok chimed in, "I remember that story. He stopped at Nob with those who were fleeing with him and asked the priest, Ahimelech, for some food. Ahimelech gave him the day old showbread. David also asked Ahimelech for a weapon, because in his haste to leave he hadn't brought one, and the priest said 'The sword of Goliath is here, but none other. You may take it,' and David responded, 'Give it to me. There is none like it.' I always wondered what that meant, 'There is none like it.' I assumed that it was just because it was big, but its size was never mentioned, just the size of Goliath's spear."

"Well," Mishimar went on, "now you know. David took it. Legend has it that later he gave it to his son Solomon and when Solomon's wives led him astray, he dedicated the sword to the Moabite god, Chemosh the conqueror, and had it placed in his shrine. Many years later before Israel was sacked, Jeremiah was led to escape with the tabernacle and Ark of the Covenant which he hid in a cave on Mt. Nebo. It was also rumored that he left Goliath's sword there too, covered and camouflaged somehow."

"It was hidden there for many years, until, one day, in the midst of a rainstorm, my grandfather, Matthan, took refuge in a cave. Inside he stumbled across some old bones. While he was looking them over in the near darkness, he thought he spied a staff wrapped in some old cloth. When he bent over to pick it up, he hit his head on something protruding from the wall, yet nearly invisible as it was covered in some sort of camouflaged material. When he removed the cloth, there was the hilt of the sword protruding from the stone sediment of the cave."

"And then what happened?" It was Hannah's turn to jump in.

Mishimar was definitely enjoying this. "When he removed the sword from the stone, it sang a note so pure that the stone crumbled all around where it had been and revealed the sheath it had been in. As he swung it around his head it was as though it kept singing, "Hane, Hane, Hane."

"Favor, the name of the sword is favor?" she questioned.

"So it would seem. Grandfather then placed it back in its sheath and brought it home."

Hannah again, "And how did it come to you?"

With another of his smiles, he answered, "That's probably a story for another time. We should pack up and get traveling." They reluctantly agreed. Mishimar helped Hanna clean and pack the dishes and in no time they were all on the road.

# Chapter 8
# On the Road

Their travel soon settled into a measured routine. Mishimar, on his amazing stallion, would scout ahead. How far ahead he scouted they were never sure, but it must have been far enough because there were never any problems. In any event, other night travelers were few and those they met seemed to pose no threat to their small band. It was to their credit that they had disguised their material prosperity and given themselves the appearance of not being wealthy without looking like they were trying not to appear wealthy. With Mishimar scouting ahead, Hannah stayed to the back. To a casual observer it might look like the three Masters were protecting her although that would have been better accomplished if she had rode in the middle. Actually, she was acting as their rear guard. In the early morning hours they used to have to begin a search for a suitable place off the road to spend the day, but Mishimar now provided that service too, as he came to them and shared that he had found a place a short distance ahead. They were soon to wonder how they ever got along without him.

They unpacked and set up their camp, Hannah then took care of the horses, while they built their small fire.

She soon had their supper prepared and they settled around the camp fire.

Mishimar began rather sheepishly, "I have a bit of an awkward question."

Suddenly he had all their attention.

"When I met Hannah, I thought it odd that you had left a woman to guard the camp, but as I held out my hand to greet her, she grasped it in such a way that I found myself on my knees and in great pain. Perhaps she might explain that?"

They all looked at her and she began, "It may be a long explanation." she said, and they all shrugged their shoulders that it did not matter. She continued, "Okay, I warned you." She took a deep breath. "I was an only child when my mother died while giving birth to me. I'm sure that my father had really wanted a boy, especially to carry on the family name, but I have done that anyway since I have never married. I did grow up as a tomboy, to please my father. He was a leader of a hundred horsemen in the cavalry, which partially explains my love of horses. He also began to teach me hand to hand combat when I was still very young, but without anyone knowing about it, as it really wasn't proper to so train a girl. I think he initially did it for my safety, teaching me self defense moves, but because I proved so adept at learning it, he taught me everything that he knew, including fighting with weapons. I was very good at it and he was secretly very proud of me. Because of his rank he had access to a private training facility and on occasion he would show me off, again secretly, to one or two of his friends. It usually went something like this. I would accompany them to their enclosed training facility, his friends wondering why he would bring a girl to their secret practice. He would simply tell them that I could be trusted. Then they paired up to spar a little with one another and when there were only the three of them, one would be left out.

So my father, sort of jokingly, would tell the third person of the party that they could spar with me. I would take a defensive stance against them, they would laugh, and then they would make a half-hearted move against me, only to find themselves flat on their back, staring at the roof. I soon had the respect of whomever my father brought over to spar. They were all sworn to secrecy, so as protect my image as a genteel maiden. It worked. We always had a good chuckle at my new sparing partner's expense and I learned things few other men even knew."

She continued, "Outside of those times I acted like a typical girl and eventually young woman. The women of our extended family trained me in the fine arts of womanhood. And I excelled at that too, so no one ever knew my father's and my secret."

Changing subjects, "Although there were few women at the stables, I was soon accepted there also. Initially it was because my father was captain of a hundred and because those who knew my secret would assure those that didn't that I could be trusted. I quickly learned that I shared a special affinity with the horses. We understood one another. This became my second secret. Those at the stables just dubbed me a "horse whisperer," but it was much simpler and deeper than that. We spoke the same language. It was a gift."

Mishimar interrupted, "Excuse me?"

When Hannah smiled she had the cutest dimples. "Yes."

He dove right in. "You are accomplished in hand to hand combat?" She nodded. He continued, "So it was no fluke when you drove me to my knees with that unique hand hold?"

Her smile deepened, "Well, I didn't know you. So, it seemed nicer than breaking your arm." He just shook his head. She asked, "Anything else?"

He was having difficulty grasping all of this. "And you talk to horses?"

She, on the other hand was enjoying this, "And listen too. Communication is both talking and listening."

Still shaking his head he asked, "How do I know you aren't just having a little bit of fun at my expense?"

Slightly coy, she offered, "I could put you on your knees again." Then she laughed.

"No," he probably wasn't supposed to blush, "That I believe. I mean about the horses."

She chuckled, "Not just horses, most animals. I could show you." She looked at the Masters and all three of them nodded. She said to them, "If you will excuse us," and to him, "We should go talk to your horse," as she stood.

Seph was smiling too as he stood. "We'll take care of the dishes."

Mishimar also stood, joined her, and they walked to the horses. He was still shaking his head in disbelief. "You are much more than meets the eye."

Her smile was in danger of becoming permanent, "I will pretend that was a compliment."

He stumbled over his words. "No, I mean, yes, I mean....Oh, I don't know what I mean. I'm usually fine around women, but you....." He left the words hanging.

"And I'll take that also as a compliment. Here we are." She put her hand out and Zillah nuzzled it. "Ah Zillah, normally I would whisper in your ear to disguise that I am actually talking to you, but so Mishimar can hear us, I will speak out loud." Zillah whinnied in response. Hannah laughed.

"Come on, he didn't say anything to you, he just whinnied." Mishimar was still stuck in his disbelief.

She looked to Mishimar, "It's not only in what he says, but how he says it. Just so you will really believe me, I will ask him to tell me something about you that I could not possibly know." She turned to Zillah and spoke to him. He whinnied again, but it was subtly different than the first time.

There was now some anticipation underlying his disbelief. "I will admit that did sound different. So, what did he say?"

Suddenly it was like she had been given a treasure. She spoke with great care and emotion. "You said you were eighteen when your father gave him to you?" He nodded. "When he did, you wept for joy and you never cry."

A tear welled up in his eye now, "But, but, but, ...that's impossible. There is no way you could know that."

The light of belief was dawning in his heart as she whispered, "Except that he just told me."

Struck with awe he stepped forward, wrapped his arms around Zillah, buried his face in his neck, and wept again for joy. When he was done he looked Zillah in the eyes, "I always knew you were special." Zillah shook his head, whinnied softly and snorted.

"He said, 'All three of us are special,' but I'm not sure he meant for me to verbalize that."

Mishimar looked at the ground, back up to Zillah, and then at Hannah as he said, "And I thought I was just hitching a ride to Jerusalem." A serious tone colored his next words, "I do have something else I would like to ask you." She nodded her assent. "Would you be amenable to some sword sparring?"

She was surprised. "We can't make a lot of noise. People might hear and that would draw attention to our journey."

He stepped back behind his saddle and pulled out of his kit two wooden swords with leather wrapped blades. "These are virtually soundless and I was wondering what on earth possessed me to bring them along."

She smiled, held out a hand, and he gave her one. They each scratched Zillah behind an ear, voiced their goodbyes to him, and walked back to the fire.

# Chapter 9
# Dance of the Swords

The three Masters had cleaned everything up from their meal and Chok and Raz were already in their tents. Seph had waited for their return from the horses.

He began, "So, now you are privy to two of Hannah's secrets."

Mishimar inquired, "There are more?"

Seph winked. "We shall see."

Hannah displayed the wooden practice sword. "We are going to do a little sparing. We'll try and not be too loud."

Seph added, "Or too long, dawn is not far off." He looked at Mishimar. "Will you be taking first watch with her?"

Mishimar smiled. "I don't know? I haven't asked her yet."

Hannah countered, "It will depend on how much I wear him out."

Seph nodded. "Then I will bid you both good night." And he turned for his tent.

Even though the morning was still chilly, Hannah removed her coat, hung it on a near bush, turned, and took a defensive posture with her sword extended.

Mishimar was afraid to ask. "Am I going to be surprised here also?"

It was her turn to wink, "Perhaps," and before he could remove his coat she attacked. She was amazing. She had obviously studied with someone of distinction as her swordplay was an elegant dance. There were absolutely no wasted movements and she seemed to be able to anticipate his. He had never faced anyone quite this wonderful and he began to imagine what it would be like if she too possessed a singing sword. What a symphony they would create. He suddenly realized he had become distracted when she deftly whacked him on the shoulder. He took a few steps back and she allowed him to disengage.

Rubbing his shoulder, he asked. "May I remove my coat now?" He found he was panting heavily.

"It looks like you may need its protection," and she winked again.

He turned his back regardless and began to shuck off his coat. "But definitely not its warmth." He was already sweating quite heavily.

"I'm glad women don't sweat, they only glisten," she grinned.

"And who on earth taught you the sword?" he asked.

She replied, "My father once captured a foreign sword master and decided that to slay him would be like destroying a beautiful stained glass window. So my father asked a favor of his general that the sword master might be allowed to live. The general would allow it as long as the master would impart to us his skill. As an artist, the sword master was grateful for the opportunity and secretly he also taught me, my third secret."

Mishimar was shaking his head again in disbelief, not at the story, but that any woman could become this skilled this young, when she began her next attack. They sparred for the better part of an hour until they both were nearly spent. Then before either of them made a move they might regret, they stopped, bowed reverently to each other, and exchanged their swords for water skins. They chatted for a few more minutes while regaining their breath and then departed to opposite ends of the camp for the first watch.

Hannah, at her end of the camp, softly began to sing the song her sword master had taught her.

*A sword is more than just a weapon*
   *more than just a tool of war,*
*A sword is more than blade and pommel*
   *of steel with finely crafted edge,*
*Extension of the warrior's arm*
   *his skill, his might, his power*
*A kiss, a breath, a soft caress*
   *expression of his mind and heart.*
*As shimmering as the angel light*
   *as gentle as a baby's sigh*
*As quick as lightning's blazing flash*
   *before the thunder's crash*
*The song it sings, the warrior's sting*
   *between the edge of life and death.*

# Chapter 10
# The Master of Languages

Their next evening's travel passed uneventful. It could have even been boring except that they all enjoyed each other's company. They filled the evening with stories and anecdotes, each Master from his own discipline, and when they were just about tired enough to stop for the day, Mishimar rode up to them with the news that he had found another good place for them to camp, just ahead.

They had settled into a comfortable routine, with each person doing their part. With a minimum of disturbances or disruptions, they were quickly ready for their meal before retiring, around the fire. Seph decided to share his story.

He began, "So, you are all probably wondering how someone becomes a Master of Languages?"

Raz answered rather seriously, "I believe that was a rhetorical question?"

Seph continued, "Yes, it was. I was an only child and a rather precocious one at that. Some would say I had the makings of a prodigy. I began speaking quite early and in complete sentences. Initially it was cute and funny, my parents showing me off to our guests, but it soon became apparent that this was no simple parlor trick. This was the real thing, whatever that meant. I also learned to read early and began to read voraciously, everything I could get my hands on. It was my good fortune to be born into the family of the curator of the largest and best library of the East. It was soon quite evident that I needed little formal education. I was very much a self starter and while my father had access to some of the best tutors in the land I quickly outstripped them one by one. Fortunately, I was of a very humble character and I say quite humbly that I still am." He chuckled. "And each of my tutors became a lifelong friend."

Raz interrupted again. "But languages, tell them how did you become intrigued with different languages?"

Seph smiled, "I was coming to that, Raz. One of my tutors, Avram, was a Hebrew mathematician and while he was teaching me my numbers decided to also teach them to me in Hebrew. When he saw how quickly I mastered that, he asked my father if he could teach me Hebrew formally. I think he also wanted to introduce me to the Hebrew god, but he didn't mention that to my father. What he did offer was to teach me Hebrew, on the side, and for free. My father could hardly pass up an offer like that and so he agreed. After my lessons in mathematics, which became shorter and shorter because of my aptitude, Avram would launch into the Hebrew lesson. He began with both the verbal and written alphabet and then used the Hebrew scriptures to teach me vocabulary and grammar. I was mesmerized by the stories I found in their scriptures, soon finding our time together passing much too quickly. I was astounded when one morning after our lesson he presented me with a copy of the first five books of Moses, the Pentateuch. He told me that when he had turned seven it had been given to him by his father and, that as a part of his early education, he had painstakingly made a copy of it by hand. Normally he would give the copy to his son on his seventh birthday, but because he had no son, only daughters, he wanted to give it to me. I wasn't even seven yet. I was deeply touched by the graciousness of his gift and, while not fully understanding its value, accepted it simply because he gave it to me. When I showed it that evening to my father, he wept for sheer joy at the blessing of the gift and that he had a son who inspired such giving. Within a month I had enough of a grasp of the language that I began reading it to myself at night. I would often come to our next lesson with questions about what I had read. This he allowed, because we now only spoke Hebrew when we were together. He would then explain his answers as best he could, but while a good mathematician and faithful Hebrew, he was not a Rabbi. What he did teach me, mostly by example, was that he was not just sharing with me concerning the Hebrew religion, but that he was offering me the possibility of a relationship with the God of the entire universe. How different this was from our gods of the East, gods that we must fear and appease. This was a God, he firmly believed the only God, who loved me as an individual and wanted me to love Him in return."

Again, it was Raz, the interruptor, speaking excitedly, "Oh, that's when you became converted to the Hebrew God?"

"Raz, Raz, Raz, calm down. I don't know that I would call it a conversion. I was nothing before, religiously, so what did I convert from?" Seph asked, "May I continue?" Raz nodded.

"One day I asked Avram, 'How can I have a relationship with your god?' He told me that I could begin by praying to Him. 'And how do I do that?'

Avram smiled and explained, 'Prayer is simply conversation with God. It is talking to God and then listening to what He has to say in return.'

I wasn't sure I understood. 'You mean talk to God like he's right here and then expecting to hear Him talk back to me?'

He nodded, still smiling, 'Yes, because He is here.'

I looked to the left and to the right and said, 'But I don't see Him.'

His gaze intensified, 'Seph, just because you can't see Him doesn't mean that He isn't here. If I go outside this room,' he pointed to the doorway, "around that wall, and talk to you. You can still hear me, even though you can't see me. It's something like that. You can talk to Him, you just can't see Him."

My astonishment deepened, 'And He will talk back to me?'

Avram quickly replied, 'Yes, if you are listening.'

I was a trifle afraid, 'What... do... I... call Him?'

His words became solemn, 'To us His name is sacred. We simply address Him as Lord.' He nodded for me to proceed.

"But what do I say?" I was still afraid.

He reassured me, 'Whatever is on your heart.'

I took a shaky breath and began, 'Lord, I have really liked reading your book, the scriptures, that Avram gave me. I would like to meet You.' And I stopped.

The strangest thing happened. It suddenly felt like someone else was there in the room with us, someone wonderful, so wonderful, that it brought tears to my eyes. I ventured further, 'Is this You?' and although I heard no actual words, I felt a resounding 'YES!' I sat there with tears slowly flowing down my cheeks. I turned to look at Avram and found there were tears flowing down his cheeks too and before I could even mouth the words, he shook his head, 'Yes.'

Avram became more of a friend than a teacher and he introduced me to some of his other friends. Soon I found myself learning Assyrian, Egyptian, and many other languages from these friends. The rest you might say is history. I became a master of these languages and the curator of the library when my father retired. I built it into the place of learning that it is today."

Seph stood up and smiled at Mishimar and Hannah, "We'll take care of the dishes if you two would like to get a little sparring in before dawn?"

Hannah looked at Mishimar, "Swords or hand to hand?"

He smiled and perhaps blushed a little, "Swords, I have a better chance at swords." And they took their leave of the Masters, collected the wooden swords, and walked to a clearing a short distance from the camp.

# Chapter 11
# Soundless Swords and Strategy

They did not begin immediately. Hannah could sense that Seph's story had made quite an impression on Mishimar, but he didn't say anything about it. He shook his head, getting rid of the lingering thoughts and handed a sword to her. They found that they were so evenly matched that sparring was really good for both of them. They were learning so much from each other. Initially, they were learning to trust each other's skill. They were also starting to explore each others strategies, and even more importantly were finding out that they really enjoyed each other's company.

While smaller and lighter than Mishimar, Hannah made up for it in speed, in the flexibility that came from a finesse learned from a master's coaching, and having practiced with so many of her father's military friends. Her offense was awesome and if he had not developed a nearly perfect defense, he would have found himself quickly over matched. He again wondered what it would be like if she wielded one of the singing swords, but this time he did not let that thought distract him. Then suddenly she performed a move he had never seen before and he found himself swordless. He stood there with his mouth wide open as she smiled.

She laughed, "What, you didn't see that coming?"

Still aghast, he muttered, "Nope. Can you show me that move again, but slowly?"

She let him pick up his sword, "If you can't defeat your opponent quickly, you can establish a rhythm of attack, pressing him hard, and then disrupt it to disarm him. Because we attack so differently, you will have to adapt it to your style, but I can show you the fundamentals." They faced each other again. "Let's do this at about half speed."

She attacked, but at only half speed and he countered at the same speed. Once she had again established a rhythm, during one of his counters she seemed to subtly change her grip and to falter. As he pressed his advantage, her grip changed again, she executed the move, and he was again disarmed. He shook his head in disbelief. "How do you do that, even at half speed?"

Her smile was almost as devastating as her swordsmanship, "Let me show you the move even more slowly." She lay down her sword and stepped around behind him, wrapped her arms around him, and put her hands on his. He was sweating, she only glistening, but her smell was intoxicating. He was finding it difficult to concentrate on the move, but he forced himself. "Once you have found the rhythm, you would normally respond to the counter, or my attack, with this grip, but you subtly shift your grip like this, as you appear to falter," and she moved his hands slightly, "thus letting your opponent overcommit in an attempt to take advantage of your fault. Then you shift your grip like this," she moved his hands again, "and execute this move," as her arms moved his. Do you want to see it again?" He nodded.

She went through it again and then realized he was enjoying their closeness a bit too much. He responded huskily, "That was amazing. You are amazing."

She disengaged. "Don't let your appreciation get in the way of our sparring or you will find out how I can also use that to my advantage.

She stepped away and picked her sword back up. "Back to half speed." She attacked. This time she let him falter and disarm her. "Again." And they did. He seemed to be getting the hang of it. "Now at full speed!" and she attacked with her normal ferocity. Once he sensed that he felt the rhythm, he faltered again and disarmed her. "One more time." And she intensified her attack even farther. This time when he faltered she didn't commit as he expected, but smacked her elbow into his shoulder, throwing him entirely off balance. She followed with a step inside that tripped him and left him sprawled on the ground.

He sat up. "I didn't see that one coming either."

"So, maybe I can show you that move tomorrow. Do you want to try some wrestling?" She offered.

"Yes!" he responded a bit too enthusiastically.

"That will have to wait too. I think you need to dunk your head in some cold water." She threw him her sword, turned, and headed towards her tent. "I'm going to turn in. Oh, and don't forget what a light sleeper I am." He could not see, but she was broadly smiling to herself.

As he walked to his tent, at the other end of the camp, he began to hum a song he had been composing.

*While wandering through a field of tangles*
*   he came upon an ancient box*
*He mused what treasure it contained*
*   perhaps 'twas only wishful thoughts*
*Regardless of the costs encountered*
*   he purchased everything there was*
*But when returning to the site*
*   he found the box was now departed*
*Replaced by just a note, "dig here".*

*Although the ground was undisturbed*
*   and nothing could be hid below*
*He took another chance at finding*
*   what thoughts betrayed his heart before*
*He dug the length, the width, and depth*

*of just a grave that he might fill*
*And as his heart was giving up*
  *his shovel clanked on something silver*
*And he unearthed a wondrous sword*

*He stood above the dirt uprooted*
  *upon a hill that he had made*
*And pulled it from an aged sheath*
  *a blade of beauty, forged of light*
*He swung it slowly, then with passion*
  *until it sang of past and future*
*Its note full blended with the wind...Hane,*
*Hane....it spoke of Favor*

# Chapter 12
# The Current Jewish King

Herod Antipater clawed his way into the position of Procurator of Judea. He showed his family, by example, that power and privilege can only be obtained and kept by the use of malice and deceit. Their family dynamics always contained internal strife, conflict, and intrigue. He mastered all of these techniques and he taught his progeny well. To begin with, they were not Jewish by birth or lineage, but they adopted the cultural customs of the Jews so as to please the people with at least a form of religion. When his sons attained sufficient age and experience he gave, first, the running of Jerusalem to his older son, Phasaelus, as its governor. Then to Herod, later called the Great, he gave Galilee. Herod Antipater manipulated an extensive network of spies and his sons both became experts at the use of their information and the incentives required to keep that information flowing: the judicious use of money and the opportunity to satisfy fleshly lusts.

When Antigonus, the last Maccabean king, together with the Parthians attacked Herod Antipater, they pressed him and his army sorely on every side. Although Herod gained a partial victory over them, they captured his youngest son, Joseph. Rather than allowing himself to be tortured and killed, Joseph committed suicide. Then the emperor, Mark Anthony, rallied to join Herod and with their combined forces they confronted Antigonus. They fought a fierce battle, but together Herod Antipater and Mark Anthony turned the tide. They captured Jerusalem and installed Herod the Great as the king of Judea.

∽

Surely becoming king signaled the end of Herod the Great's troubles. He had achieved his dream, but found it a nightmare. It is one thing to gain a throne. It is quite another to keep it. He had married Mariamne, the granddaughter of Hyrcanus, to ingratiate himself with the Maccabees. Herod had elevated her brother, Aristobulus, to the high priesthood to gain the priestly support. He thought that he had the Sanhedrin in his pocket because of all of the favors he had done for them. This should have strengthened his position as king of the Jews, but it did not.

Early one morning Herod's centurion, Anthony, knocked on his chamber doors.

"Enter." he called softly. At least he had already left his bed and dressed. His wife still slept. Anthony reluctantly entered as Herod turned from his desk. "Anthony, what is it?" Herod liked his loyalty and admired his efficiency. Anthony motioned Herod out of the room. Herod grabbed his robe and the circlet of his office, and followed him into the hallway.

Anthony shut the door behind Herod. "My lord, we have uncovered a plot against your life."

He now had Herod's full attention. "Another one, how many of these could there possibly be?" he questioned. Anthony never minced words. Herod liked that about him too.

"You have made many enemies in your ascent to the throne." He answered gravely.

"And this one?" He wished more of his subjects appreciated his rule.

"This one hits quite close to home, Sir." His eyes dropped to the floor.

"Just tell me, Anthony. You may speak freely. You know that I trust you."

"It's your wife, my king. Our spies have uncovered a plot and its roots trace back to her and her sons." Herod found it interesting that Anthony called them her sons and not Herod's.

"And the veracity of this evidence?" Herod was quite taken aback by this. He thought he loved Mariamne. He had obviously been played. "Show me this evidence!" he blustered and headed towards his palatial office.

Anthony followed him there, where a number of others already waited in attendance. Aristobulus, Mariamne's brother, the one whom Herod had elevated to the position of high priest knelt before his desk. Aristobulus had obviously been beaten, perhaps even tortured. That did not concern Herod. That this man was his wife's brother did. Two temple guards and two of his own men flanked Aristobulus. Herod sat in his rather ornate office chair which, while not his throne, would have to do for the moment.

He interwove his fingers, brought two forefingers of his intwined hands to his lips, and spoke the single word, "And?"

One of the temple guards came to attention. "Your majesty, one of your spies tipped us off to this plot against your life. It seems your wife, her brother, and her sons have been plotting this for some time. We caught them in the high priest's chambers with maps, notes, and a stored cache of weapons." He motioned to Aristobulus.

"The boys escaped and we are hunting them down, but this one has confessed to everything."

Herod spat the words out, "Take him to the dungeon and let me know when the boys have joined him."

Anthony spoke up, "And your wife, Sir?"

Herod smiled rather slyly, "Let her think everything is still fine, for the time being."

They hauled Aristobulus to his feet, turned, and dragged him out of Herod's presence. Anthony remained, "Sir, if I might make a suggestion?"

Anger, disappointment, betrayal, many emotions all clamored for Herod's attention. He spoke curtly, "Yes, Anthony, what else?"

"What if we could discover these plots sooner?" he ventured.

"And how do you propose that we do that?" Herod said flatly.

"One of your father's wizards is particularly adept at obtaining this kind of information. As a master of the black arts he is privy to things we can't even imagine," Anthony continued.

"It didn't help my father much." Herod stated matter of factly.

"That would be because your father did not make use of him. Your father feared his power."

Knowing his father that made sense. "And you think I should consult this wizard?" He did trust Anthony, did he not?

"It might prove prudent to use all available resources if we are to allow your reign to prosper." Anthony smiled.

"And the name of this wizard?" Herod too began to smile.

"His name is Nebo and I have seen him do amazing things. He is no simple charlatan and neither is his son, Nesher." Anthony added.

"And do I need to fear his power?"

"Let's just say it would also be prudent to have a healthy respect of him and his power." Anthony said seriously.

"OK, bring him to me." he commanded.

"Sir, I might also suggest as a gesture of good faith that you go to him. It would be interpreted not as a sign of weakness, but as a sign of respect, the respect that your father never gave him."

Herod only let a few people talk to him as near equals. Anthony was one of those few. He shook his head yes. "I agree, set up this meeting," and turned to the paperwork on his desk.

Anthony nodded, bowed slightly, turned and quickly left the king's office, his steps full of purpose.

# Chapter 13
# The Master of Religions

The days grew shorter and the nights longer as the Masters, Hannah, and Mishimar traveled through the autumn and into winter. They decided to switch from traveling at night to traveling during the day and agreed to spend some time in the next town restocking their provisions. Although disguised, the three Masters could easily blow the "simple travelers" cover story with their vocabulary, so, Mishimar and Hannah did most of the talking and negotiations for the supplies. Mishimar carried the purse. Since not many people would attempt to rob a swordsman. Without appearing to have too much money, they obtained lodging for the night in the local inn, purchasing an entire floor, complete with private dining and sitting rooms. By dusk they sat together for a hot meal, prepared for and delivered to them by the inn's cook. As she left, Chokmah spoke up.

"It is interesting how fortune has smiled on all of us and brought us together for this amazing adventure. Raz, do you remember how surprised you were to find out that Seph serves only the one God of the Hebrews? In the East we serve many gods. I was raised in a priestly family that served Qingu, the possessor of the three tablets of destiny. According to legend, the god Abzu and goddess

Taimat joined together to produce the offspring Qingu. When Marduk, another god, murdered Abzu, Taimat gave Qingu the three tablets of destiny to confirm him as the supreme deity. My father served that supreme deity as priest, but as I grew up, I became acquainted with a seemingly lesser deity called Enlil, the god of the wind."

Chok continued, "As children, we used to play the game of rock, paper, knife where rock breaks knife, paper covers rock, and knife cuts paper. Each one can defeat another, but none of them can defeat them all. But what about the elemental force of the wind? With the four elements of earth, wind, fire, and water; it is not about who defeats whom, but about cooperating, one with the other, to produce life. So, for me, it was not about who was the most powerful or supreme, but who was the most mysterious force in the process of life. For me, that was the wind."

A faraway look now glazed over his eyes. "I was in the middle of my studies one day when I came across the Hebrew's word for wind, Ruach. I found that it also could be translated as breath, spirit, and even in some instances as life itself. It also seemed to have the almost human qualities of personality ascribed to it as it acted throughout the Hebrew scriptures. I had met Seph during my studies and consulted him often, as my searching had taken me to other languages. It was on one of those occasions, while exploring the words for wind, that Seph introduced me to something, someone else, called Chayeem, the Tree of Wind. I was astonished. How could the three elements of Earth, Wind, and Water combine into a Tree that pulsated, breathed, the very essence of Life itself."

He smiled endearingly towards Seph. "Seph explained to me that while God's name was too wonderful or sacred to be verbalized, he had discovered another name that he could use, which was more personal than simply calling Him, Lord. That name was Chayeem and as the Tree of Wind, He seemed the embodiment of all I had been searching for too. Therefore, we began to meet together to study, contemplate, meditate, discuss, and even worship Chayeem as the personification of the one God. This eventually led us to discovering the ceremony of the One Tree that we now celebrate weekly."

Mishimar asked, "So, what about you, Raz, how did you join this trio?"

Raz replied, "That is probably a story for another evening. We should try to get some rest if we are to successfully transition to traveling during the day." The other two Masters nodded in agreement and rose to leave.

Mishimar looked at Hannah. "Perhaps we will sit and chat a bit longer?" Seph winked at her behind Mishimar's back as they left.

She questioned. "I don't suppose there is a place to spar at this time of night?"

Mishimar put his elbows on the table, folded his hands together, and placed his chin on them. "I guess verbal sparring will have to do for this evening." and he smiled, "I was wondering how you became associated with this group?"

She smiled in return. "You haven't had enough stories for one evening?"

He shook his head. "No."

And she began her answer, "As you have probably gathered by now, although you haven't heard Raz's story, all three of these gentlemen are highly skilled in what they each do." Mishimar nodded his tacit agreement. "My father had met Seph on a number of occasions when he acted as translator for the prisoners we had captured during our many conquests. My father was not only impressed with his skills in language, but also with his character and his demeanor. In my father's quest to round out my motherless upbringing, he asked Seph if he would consider taking me on as a student. It wasn't that he was disappointed to have a secret female warrior for a daughter, he wanted to round out my education, even though that too would have to be completed in secret."

"What?" Mishimar exclaimed, "You have been educated too?"

Hmmmm, soon she would have no secrets left from her new friend at all. "Yes, I am afraid you will find me your equal in many areas. Seph had been instrumental in my learning from the captured sword master, so he knew he had a unique pupil already. He translated for us until I knew enough of the sword master's language and his sword skills to no longer require his aid. Yet he had continued to attend our secret night sessions, often adding his own comments afterwards. Those were days of hard work and not much sleep that allowed he and I to grow very close. He became like a second or surrogate father to me. " She stopped to sooth her dry throat with a drink. That helped her to continue.

"Will you never cease to amaze me?" Smiled Mishimar admiringly.

"I hope not," returning his smile coyly, "a bit of mystery is always one of a woman's greatest weapons. When I reached a marriageable age, my father began to worry about my protection when he was out on campaign. One evening when Seph was with us, after I had prepared supper and my father assumed I was busy with the dishes, he asked Seph if he would consider acting as my god-father when he was absent. Seph was visibly touched and said he could think of no greater privilege. My father said he would have to ask me, but Seph nodded towards the kitchen doorway where I silently stood, visibly shaken myself. I ran and embraced them both, weeping deeply touched that my father loved me enough to plan for my future, and achingly grateful that Seph would want that responsibility. Oh, another secret! I don't cry very often, either!"

Mishimar nodded his head in understanding. "When did Seph find out about you and horses?"

Her eye might have glistened with a tear or it may just have been the light. "A few years ago, my father was killed in battle. Later that evening, Seph and I were with the sword master in the training facility when the stable master burst in on us."

"Hannah, come quickly! Your father's horse has returned without him and is causing quite a ruckus at the stables!" he stammered.

She continued, "I nearly threw my sword at the sword master and ran back to the stable with the stable master. There in the middle of the arena, warily encircled by a number of groomsmen, my father's horse, Midnight, bucked and whirled and pawed the ground, nearly mad with emotion. 'Opelyeem!' I yelled his name commandingly. Fortunately over the commotion, he heard me and looked in my direction. 'Come!' I shouted as I gestured forcibly with a downward slash of my hand to my side. He stopped abruptly as though I had cold-cocked him. He tottered a moment where he stood, and then panting heavily, hung his head, walked to my side, and collapsed at my feet. I don't know if you have ever heard a horse cry, but it is a terribly painful thing. Through his broken sobs he told me what had happened. He and my father had fought together for years and they were both incredible warriors and nearly invincible together, but in this instance an arrow that neither of them had seen or heard in the clamor of battle, had struck my father between the plates of his armor and unhorsed him. My father had been engaging the enemy's champion and the two men and horses had fought to a standstill when the arrow struck. Before Midnight could counter and stand to protect my father, their champion had leapt from his horse and engaged my father on the ground. Wounded, my father still put up an incredible fight as the two horses also fought to protect their riders. Weakened with loss of blood and the powerfully ferocious attack of the enemy, my father was finally slain. Then, as though time stood still, the enemy champion, rather than desecrating my father's body or chopping off his head as a trophy, honored him by picking up his sword, whiping it clean, and sheathing it in the scabbard on Midnight's saddle as he stood transfixed at my father's death. Their champion then turned, mounted his own horse, and rode away."

Mishimar did not know what to say, but now a tear glistened on his own cheek.

"The spell broken, Midnight stood on his hind legs and screamed to the sky in agony and grief, and then left the field in the shame that he had been unable to protect my father. As the enemy's champion rode away, the battle stopped and the two armies disengaged. Midnight galloped all the way back home in the madness of his grief. I then fell to the ground with him, my arms around his neck and we wept together until he was quieted enough that I could release him into the care of the stable master. I assured them both that I would return soon. Seph took me back to his home and I shared with him all that Midnight had told me. That's how he found out that I talk to horses. I have lived with him ever since, as his daughter and friend. For the sake of appearances we pretend that I am his house-keeper and the community seems to have accepted that."

Mishimar realized with some embarrassment that sometime during the last part of her story he had reached out and taken her hand. He looked down at their hands, then up into her eyes, and reluctantly let go of her hand.

"Thank you for sharing that with me," he whispered huskily.

"You're welcome," she breathed softly. "Thanks for listening, but it's time for bed." She stood and walked hesitantly to her room. His eyes longingly followed her.

Mishimar sat there at the table for some time, his thoughts whirling, his emotions conflicted. What was happening to him? He had never met people quite like these. The three Masters amazed him with their stories, their conviction, their abandonment to this quest to find the "Promised One." Then there was Hannah. He had met many women in his life, some beautiful, some strong, courageous, and capable, but never one that he would have truly considered his equal in every way. And here she was, with still so much mystery about her. He needed to take care or he might fall in love with her, although he never thought falling in love possible. No, he controlled his own heart, his destiny. Yet suddenly he seemed in over his head, beyond his depth, swallowed up in a story he did not fully understand. He found it a bit frightening, but also exciting. And what of Chayeem? His parents had believed and he had thought he did too, but did he really believe like these did? They actually talked to Him and believed that He talked back to them. Could a personal, loving God exist? He pondered giving it a try. He suddenly felt silly, like a young child. He did not feel bad, he just had not felt like this in a long time. He took his first halting steps, "Chayeem... I thought I knew You, but maybe I have just known about You. I don't think that I have ever actually met You. If that is truly possible, tonight, I would like to." and he waited. Suddenly across from him sat an old man. He did not appear old and weak, he looked old and exceedingly strong. Astonished, Mishimar could not speak.

The old man did. "I am Uriel. I thought it time that we met, at least briefly. What would it take for you to know beyond a shadow of a doubt that Chayeem was real? It's an interesting question, one that He would like to answer." And he was gone.

Mishimar mused, *"And what would be the answer to that question?"* His question wasn't particularly directed anywhere, he was just thinking about what Uriel had said. But suddenly it was as if he had asked the question and the answer was there, the palatable presence of someone more real than reality itself and it felt as wonderful as Seph had described, so wonderful it brought tears to his eyes. "So this is You, Chayeem?" and he felt his own resounding, "YES!" He sat there for a while, engulfed in His presence and then finally said, "Thank you." The presence receded and he got up and went to his bed, feeling like he had finally found home and family once again.

# Chapter 14
# Master of the Mysteries

Traveling during the day created its own set of problems. Like the increased interaction with other people which made it more difficult to keep up the appearance of three simple travelers who had employed a cook and a bodyguard. They let their story expand into three merchants thus explaining the extra pack animals, and it seemed to be generally accepted. To keep to themselves also became more difficult, but Mishimar regularly found them a campsite about a half hour off the roads. He succeeded again this particular evening and after supper, while Hannah cleaned up, Raz began to share his story.

∞

Raz sat up a little straighter, "My story, while not as exciting as Seph's or Chok's is still a good story." He smiled. "My family seemed neither special or particularly unique. We were a pretty typical Eastern family: Mom, Dad, two and a half kids, and a dog."

Chok smiled as he got the opportunity to interrupt for a change. "Who was the half of a kid?"

Raz chuckled, "It was just a mathematical expression of the normal/average family. My father was a cloth merchant, so while not wealthy, we were well off enough.

I was not especially popular in school, but not an outcast either. Again, like my family I was sort of nondescript. I did excel in mathematics and what passed for science, especially working with the mixing of potions. Some might describe it as sorcery, but it included no black magic. I became apprenticed to a healer that some might have called a witch, but Rachel was just a wise woman adept with herbs and poultices. She seemed happy to have the company of someone who could remember a formula or prescription....and follow directions. Rachel did teach me magic. Although most of it was simple slight of hand, there were some other tricks too which I used mostly to entertain children. Together Rachel and I enjoyed the thrill of discovery. On the back of her property she maintained a house which might have been considered a primitive laboratory. We spent many hours back there concocting some unimaginable things. My parents didn't seem to care as Rachel presented herself as harmless enough, I was earning a little money, and I wasn't getting into trouble. They considered that successful."

Chok interrupted again, not willing to pass up an opportunity, "What does all this have to do with 'the mysteries'?"

Raz shook his head back and forth in disbelief as Chok had his interruption revenge, "What are 'the mysteries'? They are simply the things you don't understand, but I do. If I understand a lot of things that other people don't understand, then I am a Master of the Mysteries. I also loved research. Rachel would often send me to the library to find out information about some obscure plant or other ingredient. There I encountered Seph. He was already a Master of Languages, yet I never feared to approach him. I don't think I ever saw Seph turn someone away, even if their question seemed trite or silly. To him there were no stupid questions, just poor answers and he was always ready to help the truly inquisitive find a good answer to their question. He helped me on occasions too numerous to count and we became friends."

Raz took a drink of water while he and Seph smiled at one another, then his tone turned reverent. "Seph introduced me to Chayeem. One afternoon after helping me find the reference to a particularly obscure herb, he asked me to share tea with him. As we sat at the table he asked me, 'What would you describe as the basic ingredient to life?'

Ah, the mystery of life, a question I had often pondered. 'Well, we have the four elements of earth, wind, fire, and water. Is one greater than the others?'

Seph pulled out a scroll of the first book of the Hebrew scriptures called 'Genesis', opened it up, and read to me the story about a shepherd named Moses, who while walking one day in the mountains encountered a 'burning bush', a bush burning yet not consumed by the fire. Moses turned aside to see this marvel and a voice spoke to him out of the fire saying 'Take off your sandals, the ground you are standing on is holy'. It seemed this was a physical representation of God at least for that moment. The burning bush combined the elements of earth, fire, and water. Then Seph told me about another tree, one that had been present in the garden of Delight, a Tree of Wind called Chayeem. Right there, having tea around his table, he introduced me to Chayeem, the greatest of mysteries."

Mishimar raised his hand, Raz acknowledged it. "You don't have to raise your hand Mishimar."

"I know," he said, "but it seemed a bit less disruptive way to interrupt you." as he smiled at Chok.

"That's fine." said Raz, "I was pretty much done."

"Well," continued Mishimar, "I met Chayeem the other night at the inn."

Seph stood and took a step towards him, his hand extended, "Welcome formally then into our little group." The rest of them broke into smiles, especially Hannah.

And there, just beyond the fire sat the old man Mishimar had just met the other night, Uriel, the angel in his human form. "And I too offer my congratulations." He paused a moment. "I would like to bring up a topic for our discussion."

Raz questioned, "I thought angels brought messages not discussions."

The old man smiled, "As you are all aware, you are a rather special collection of people. To you I will bring a discussion. We are almost to Jerusalem. We need a plan on how you are to proceed once we get there."

It was Seph's turn, "Do you have a recommendation for our discussion?"

The old man nodded, "Yes, I do. I would recommend against a direct approach to Herod, who believes that he is the king of the Jews."

Seph replied, "Why should we go to Herod at all? Isn't that a bit risky?"

"Yes." Chok added, "Herod seems to have combined political and religious power into a single tyrannical fist, from what I have heard."

"How have you heard that?" Raz questioned.

"I was asking people casually in the inn's tavern." He continued, "It seems Herod has had the help of Cesear. They said he has allied himself with the Sanhedrin, and that until recently his brother-in-law served as high priest."

Seph interjected, "So, he might not be too pleased that we search for the new king?"

Uriel replied, "Definitely not! However, I'm told," and he pointed upward like Chok, "Herod holds some relevant information."

Mishimar entered the discussion, "What if we just started asking around, trying to find out any information concerning a new king, beginning at whatever inn where we stay?"

Hannah added, "And I could ask among the woman. There is usually quite a lot of information available at the city wells. If we asked around enough, the word will eventually get to Herod, and he will probably send for us himself."

Uriel stood, "I think that might work."

He stood up and so did Mishimar, who addressed him tentatively. "Sir, do you have one of the singing swords?".

Suddenly Uriel appeared a full eight cubits tall and as he withdrew the sword from its sheath musical wonder engulfed them. "Does that answer your question?"

Mishimar drew his own sword and it matched Uriel's with its own harmony. He ventured, "Could we spar together sometime?"

Uriel, although terrible to behold, smiled hugely, "I'm afraid that if we did that, you would no longer be able to remain incognito. Perhaps, one day when this adventure is complete we may both have the pleasure. I look forward to that day." Looking at the rest of the troop he promised, "I will still be with you, but no longer visible." And he disappeared out of their sight.

It took a moment for them all to recover, but when they had, Hannah walked over and embraced Mishimar chastely. "I'm so glad you too have met Chayeem." The rest nodded their agreement and there might have been a tear in Mishimar's eye as he mentally and emotionally exhausted said, "We should all head off to our beds?"

# Chapter 15
# The Wizard

This small man of indeterminate age, would never be mistaken as weak or frail. From every pore of his being there exuded a dark elemental power. He often stood at Herod's right hand, always close, whether in the throne room or the dining room. His name was Nebo and he was the king's most trusted wizard.

∽

"Nebo." Herod spoke with dark affection, "Remind me how we met."

"Your Majesty," in a voice like a slow caress, "You had developed an infected wound for which there seemed no cure. It irritated you constantly. No one knew of this, not your wife, nor your concubines, no trusted advisor, no one, except the young Sumerian serving girl who collected your soiled linens. One day she haltingly whispered that she thought she knew who could help. You didn't believe her, and suspecting some plot, demanded to know if she thought to gain something. She said, "No!" in such a tone that it almost costs her head.

"What, what could possibly help me?" you said sarcastically.

"The Wizard, Nebo." she bravely replied.

Nebo continued, "Surprised at her courage and loyalty, you spared her life, and sent for me."

"Ah yes, I remember," Herod mused. "She did rather impress me and I had you brought forth. However, I did not tell you for what reason."

"That's true, my Lord," Nebo continued, "but my god, Marduk, the god who reveals secrets, had already told me about you and your plight and together he and I restored you."

"And having done me this great service," Herod smiled up to him, "What did you ask of me in return?"

"Simply to serve you as I serve my god, continually and completely."

"And that you are doing, that you are doing." Herod chuckled, as he reached over and patted Nebo's hand, the one that held his staff of power.

Herod scratched his chin, "I seem to recall that before this occasion, my centurion Anthony, had told me about you. During the betrayal of my wife, he said you could help frustrate the plans of my enemies. I think I even sent him to arrange a meeting with you."

"Yes, you did, Lord," Nebo remembered the story well. He had later been told what had happened. "But your wife was having him followed and attempted to assassinate him before he reached me. In the aftermath of putting down her insurrection you all forgot your earlier intention."

"Well," the king smiled, "you have more than made up for my lapse since. With your help we have been able to nip every other attempted coup in the bud."

"Yes," Nebo said feigning humility, "Marduk has enlightened us to a number of plots early enough to render them ineffective. Speaking of which, I must beg your leave. It seems that we may have another plot formulating."

That perked the king up. "By all means, whatever you must do."

&#x223A;

Nebo left the king and retreated to his own dark chambers and his underground temple of sorcery. There he had a black altar dedicated to his god Marduk. He never entered there without a sacrifice. This time was special. Through his dark contacts he had secured a still- born child from delivery that morning. He brought the corpse and lay it on the altar. He prepared to disembowel it when a blazing light halted his hand. Before him stood a towering being of indescribable beauty.

He fell to his knees, "My god, Marduk?"

The being spoke and it seemed all the air was sucked out of the room. "I have many names, that one will do for now. I have something for you, Nebo. Seven singing swords were forged for the higher gods. I brought two of the gods and their swords with me in my war against the heavens. I want to give one of those swords to your son, Nesher. Bring him to me and slay him on this altar!"

The being disappeared, so did the corpse. *"What!"* he screamed inside of his head, *"Slay my son on the altar?"* It made no sense. How was Marduk going to give his son the singing sword if he had slain him on his black altar? Unfortunately, he knew the power of Marduk. He was not just the god of Secrets and Sorcery. He was also called "the Devourer of Souls." Nebo had to do what the Being commanded or suffer the consequences. He went and found his son, Nesher.

Nesher was a warrior, the best fighter his father had ever seen, and he said that without bias. He fought with amazing skill, hand to hand, or with any weapon in his hands. However, Nesher had never accompanied his father to the underground temple. Still he trusted his father implicitly. After all, blood was blood. Nebo had never seen his son afraid, never even a little bit and it was not that Nesher was simply naive. He seemed born devoid of a fear reflex. He followed his father down the stairs and along a hallway until they came to large ornate door covered in occult signs and symbols.

Nesher looked at his father. "Where does this lead, father?"

There was a tear in his father's eye, "To a place so secret and sacred that I have never shared it with another living soul, but tonight I share it with you."

Nesher was taken aback. He knew some of his father's dark secrets, but that this had been kept from him was a surprise. That his father now sought to share it with him touched him deeply. A tear glistened his own eye and he never cried. "Thank you for trusting me with this." he spoke hoarsely as he pointed to the door.

Nebo touched the door with his staff and the way opened. They walked into the darkened chamber with its black stone altar. "Son, I need you to disrobe and lay on the altar." Without hesitation he did so. Neither did Nebo hesitate as he thought *"Perhaps Marduk will resurrect my son, Nesher, from the dead and then give him the sword."* Nebo withdrew his sacred knife and raised it above his head, but before he could bring it down, dazzling light filled the chamber and the Being stood there once again.

He spoke, "Now I know I can fully trust you, for you would sacrifice to me your son, your only son." He brought forth a sword in a scabbard. When he withdrew it from the scabbard, Nebo saw no blade, just the hilt. The sound it made brought pain to every fiber of Nebo's body. It took all of his strength to remain standing. Nesher, on the altar, seemed unaffected. Marduk held the sword forth to Nebo, palms up, pommel in one hand and the "no blade" seeming to rest in his other. "This is the sword Balak. Take it!"

With all the courage and strength he could muster, Nebo reached out and grasped the hilt of the sword, sliding his hand under the place where the blade should be. As soon as Marduk released the sword into Nebo's hands the blade became visible to Nebo's eyes. He almost dropped it, so suddenly did the pain disappear.

The Being hissed, "The Hebrews circumcise their male children as a sign of dedication to their puny god. Instead of slaying Nesher, you will circumcise him in dedication to me." It was a command. It didn't matter what Nebo thought, he had to obey. It should have been cumbersome to do with a sword what is usually done with a small knife, but to Nebo it felt like the sword had a mind of its own. Even though Nesher understood the coming ceremony he still evidenced no fear. He did not even flinch as Nebo began. There seemed no pain, there was no blood, as though the blade cauterized the wound it created. To Nesher it all seemed as magic, since he could not see the blade of the sword. When Nebo finished, Marduk spoke, "Nesher, you now belong to me! Nebo, re-sheath the sword." Nebo did. "Nesher, stand and then kneel before your father." Nesher obeyed. "Nebo, you may now give your son Balak." Nebo extended the sword, in its scabbard, on his palms, to his son. Nesher took the sword, still kneeling.

∞

Suddenly a wall to the left opened and the room behind it illuminated. Marduk gestured towards the room. "Here and only here will you practice with Balak until the day I send you to destroy my enemies," and the Being vanished.

Nesher tied the sword to his belt and walked into the room, which appeared arrayed as a sparring chamber, followed by his father. At the far end of it stood two guards and a prisoner. The prisoner appeared to be a foreign warrior in excellent health and peak physical condition. They unshackled him and handed him a sword. Nesher wondered why he did not immediately attack the guards, but rather swung the sword back and forth to get the feel of it. He took two steps toward Nesher and assumed a defensive stance. Nesher drew Balak and nearly cried out from the sheer physical pleasure and power that he felt from it. As he swung Balak, he felt his body and soul align with his eternal destiny. Although the prisoner proved an excellent swordsman he could not compete with Nesher and his implement of death. Nesher dispatched him quickly.. The two guards dragged the corpse out of the chamber as Nesher wiped the blood, he surprisingly found, off the blade. He re-sheathed it and placed it in the receptacle on the table that stood off to his right which seemed made for the sword. He turned, embraced his father, and together they walked out of the chamber, Nebo's arm around his warrior son's shoulder.

# Chapter 16
# The Other Fallen Sword

Hannah had spent much of the day at the city wells asking if anyone knew about the new king that had been born. She heard a few rumors about shepherds seeing angels and discovering a baby born in the feeding trough of an animal shelter in a small town a few stadia away. That did not sound much like the birth of a king, except the angel part of it. Meanwhile, the Masters and Mishimar did the same throughout the market places. They heard similar stories, but nothing more. The angel part of the story might be significant, but why would the next king be born inconspicuously in a stable somewhere?

That evening after supper and sharing their findings for the day, Hannah cautiously asked Mishimar a question she had pondered for some time, "Do you know what happened to the singing sword that fell with the other Nephilim?"

A graveness that they rarely saw settled over Mishimar's face. "Yes, although most of that knowledge is either legend or mere speculation."

He took a ragged breath and sighed deeply, "There were numerous giants during the time of David, before and after he was king. Some say that is why he stopped at the stream on his way to slay Goliath and picked up five smooth stones. There were at least four other known giants and there was no assurance that Goliath's promise, 'If you slay me we will become your slaves' would be honored or if David would have to fight the others. He also might have just been unsure he could drop Goliath with a single stone. In any event, David battled a number of the other giants after he became king. Some of those battles are recorded in your ancient Scriptures. In one of those battles he faced the giant Ishbi-benob. David and his armies were battling the Philistines again when Ishbi-benob took the field. We don't know how tall he was, whereas Goliath was over six cubits, but his name can be translated as 'dwelling in the heights.' We do know that the weight of his spear was only half of Goliath's. Still that made it an impressive weapon. It is curious to note a number of other things in the story. Ishbi-benob was intent on killing David, who was the "only" giant killer at that point. David was growing weary from the fighting, and Ishbi-benob was fighting using a 'new sword.' The word 'sword' is not actually in the text. The chronicler couldn't tell what it was, only that Ishbi-benob was wielding it 'like a sword,' I suppose. It doesn't say what David was fighting with either, but it may have been the sword he took from Goliath."

Hannah interjected, "So, what was Ishbi-benob fighting with?"

Mishimar's graveness had left, as he began to enjoy the narrative, "Legend has it that the other archangel that had fallen in the rebellion with Halel also had a liaison with a Moabite woman and that the off-spring of that illicit relationship was Ishbi-benob. Although we have no record of the great deeds that he did, like Goliath's slaying of the Ariel, it is said that he performed some amazing exploits against the enemies of Moab to prove his right to be worshipped as a demigod. The Angel of Indescribable Beauty also graced the ceremony of Ishbi-benob's maturity and bequeathed to him his father's singing sword. That sword, having been so long dedicated to the service of darkness, no longer reflected light but sucked it all in so as to appear virtually invisible. It was only when drawn, when it sung its discordant harmony, that it could be perceived at all except by the person wielding it. What the angel handed Ishbi-benob appeared to be a sword, but when the angel commanded him to take the sword and he drew it out, all of the guests at the ceremony fell to the ground in convulsions at its discord. The invisible blade is called Balak, the void."

Hannah spoke again, "So the battle between David and Ishbi-benob may have been a battle of two singing swords?"

"Which would explain why the text says that David, Israel's champion, was growing weary." confirmed Mishimar.

"And then what happened?" Hannah was almost pleading.

"It seems that Ishbi-benob was so intent on his purpose to slay David that Abashai, the brother of Joab, David's general, was able to sneak in a stroke and slay Ishbi-benob. The legends say that the invisible sword became Abashai's reward for slaying the giant and that when he and his brother left the employ of the king, they took the sword with them. From there it fell into obscurity."

"And that's the end of the story of the second sword?" Hannah asked.

"Not quite." he answered. "A few months ago, in my travels, I came across a wandering prophet. When I met him, he acted like I had just slapped him. He quickly recovered his composure, stepped forward, gripped my shirt, and said, 'You will meet the void in the hand of the enchanter and his intent will be to destroy you too.' Not particularly comforting. Perhaps we can speak of something better before we all go to bed."

Hannah reluctantly left the story unfinished at that point. What had the prophet meant? She had so many questions stirring in her head and heart, but they spoke of other things before they went off to their respective beds for their much needed sleep.

Suddenly, in the middle of the night, came an incessant knocking at the door to their suite of rooms. Seph opened the door and a number of guards pushed their way into the room and made way for their centurion. Mishimar stepped instinctively in front of Hannah. He had his sword in his hand albeit still sheathed. She pushed him aside to gain room to maneuver. The centurion spoke curtly, not a request, but a command. "Please excuse the late hour, but the king requires your presence! Dress quickly and we will escort you to him."

How do you dress for an audience with the king and yet maintain the ruse of being simple merchants? They did the best they could, Hannah in a deep blue muslin and the men in the only clean clothes that were not travel-worn. When Mishimar stepped out of his room, he was girded with his singing sword.

The centurion's hand went immediately to the hilt of his own sword, "You cannot bring a weapon into the presence of the king!" He obviously commanded the situation.

Mishimar countered, "Well, I'm sure not leaving it here!"

The centurion held out his hand, "Let me see it!" With reluctance, Mishimar unbelted it and handed it to him. The centurion took it and partially withdrew it. His eyes widened. He stared intently into Mishimar's eyes, a look of deep appreciation on his face. "This is a wondrously fine blade. You have my word that I will take care of it for you." It was difficult for him not to covet the blade, but as an officer his oath was rock solid. Once they left the suite of rooms and the inn, the guards formed around them to protect them and conveyed them to the palace.

# Chapter 17
# Before the King

They marched to the palace without incident, though the late evening hour held a certain chill. Herod designed his palace to intimidate and it succeeded. The polished stone and marble spotlessly gleamed with all the lit torches. Gold and silver accents and lavish furnishings were everywhere. The soldiers left them in a large antechamber, complete with a servant, who obviously only recently awakened, offered them sweetmeats, fresh fruit, and beverages, all of which they declined. After a respectable wait, to show them their place, the centurion returned to usher them into the king's court. He no longer held Mishimar's sword.

Sitting on his throne, amidst extravagant splendor, but with only a handful of retainers, sat Herod the Great, Mishimar's sword across his knees. "Who claims this sword?" Herod demanded.

Mishimar stepped forward and bowed slightly. "I am Mishimar and it is mine, your Majesty," he calmly said.

The king looked him up and down slowly, trying to match the man to the blade he held. "And where did you come by such an extraordinary weapon?"

Mishimar stood unflinchingly under the king's evaluation, "My father handed it down to me and he had received it from his father."

"Do you have any idea of its value?" the king questioned.

"Sir, it means much more to me than any monetary value that could be attached to it." Mishimar replied forthrightly.

"Anthony." The centurion stepped forward as the king held out the sword, "Take very good care of this while it is in my palace. It is a weapon fit for a god, let alone a king." Herod handed off the sword and then looked back to Mishimar. "I don't suppose there is any way I could persuade you to part with it?"

Mishimar shook his head, "No, Sir, not as long as I have breath." Then he somewhat regretted the way he had said it.

"And who accompanies a man with such a sword?" inquired the king.

"My companions are the Eastern Masters of Languages, Mysteries, and Religions. May I introduce Seph, Raz, and Chok." They each stepped forward and bowed as he introduced them. Then Mishimar added with a small smile, "And their cook, Hannah, your Majesty."

"They do not look like Masters of anything, but then she looks like much more than just a cook." He smiled, narrowing his eyes.

"Looks can be deceiving, Sir. We have traveled a long distance without any problems, partly through that deception." Mishimar continued.

"And why have you come into my kingdom?" the king asked.

Seph now stepped forward. "I am certain you know that, your Majesty." he paused, "I mean no disrespect, but we seek the "new" king of the Jews. We have come to worship him."

Herod bristled at that, but tried not to show it. He slowly stood. "I am the king of the Jews."

Seph continued, "Currently, yes, but we have been led here to meet a child that has been born...."

"Led here? Led here, by whom?" The king noticeably held a tight rein on his emotions.

Seph looked at the others almost pleadingly. "His.... star appeared to us in the East and.... we have followed that star here."

The king relaxed, "A star appeared, you are following that star, and it has led you here? You must think me a fool!"

Now it was Seph's turn to smile. "Forgive me, your Majesty, but according to our studies and our traditions, such a star would only appear to herald the birth of a very great person and we have traveled many months to find him."

The king abruptly turned to his centurion, "Anthony, take them back out there!" and he pointed to the ante-chamber.

Marcus took them back to the chamber and shrugged off their worried looks, and left them standing there while he returned to the throne room.

Herod felt disturbed. He called for the magicians, sorcerers, priests, advisors, all of them and then left the throne room. Because of the hour, it took some time for them all to assemble, and then more time as they argued about who should get to stand where in his throne room. Nebo and his son entered last. They went and stood on the king's dais, just behind the right shoulder of his throne. The king re-entered and they all bowed. The king sat and spoke slowly and deliberately, "Some men have come from the East seeking a new king." He spoke the next words with menace, emphasizing each word. "Where is this new king?"

Un-nerved, they looked at one another fearfully. One ventured, "We have no king but you, Oh Herod!" Many of them nodded.

"Silence!" he shouted. "I asked you a question! Where is this new king that was born? "

One of the priests, a scholar in the Hebrew scriptures, stepped forward and said, "My Lord, our scriptures prophesy that he will be born in Bethlehem. It says:

Bethlehem, while you seem but a little one
  you are far from insignificant
For from you shall emerge a ruler
  who will gather all my people together
For he is sent from of old..."

Herod interrupted him, "Bethlehem, this king will be born in Bethlehem?"

"So it would seem, my Lord," the priest responded.

"When? When will he be born? Tell me, tell me!" His emotions appeared about to slip their leash.

They all looked at one another confused. Nebo leaned over and whispered something in the king's ear.

"Get out, get out! All of you!" the king screamed. Then he spoke more calmly to Anthony, "Bring those men and that woman back in here." Marcus went out of the throne room to the antechamber, and brought the five of them back into the king's presence. The king stared at them, "When was this child born? When did his star first appear to you?"

Seph again became their spokesman, "It has been almost two years since the star first appeared to us."

A smile slowly spread across the king's face as he spoke to them calmly, "Go to Bethlehem and find the child. When you have found him, return to me and tell me that I may recognize him." Nebo leaned over and whispered in his ear again and the king amended his words, "and that I may also come and worship him." And the king dismissed them.

# Chapter 18
# Towards Bethlehem

Once outside the throne room, they asked Anthony, "Why is the king sending us to Bethlehem?"

He looked at them in confusion and then realized that they had not been in the room for the prior discourse. "The king assembled all his magicians, sorcerers, priests, advisors, and asked where this new king would be born. Eleazar, the priest, is also a scholar and quoted from their Hebrew scriptures an ancient prophecy that said the king would be born in Bethlehem."

Anthony led them all the way out of the palace, to the courtyard of the king, and then asked hesitantly. "Mishimar, before I return this wondrous sword to you, I ask that I might swing it a few times?"

Mishimar looked at his friends who just shrugged their shoulders. The decision was his and his alone, except that Hannah smiled and nodded yes. That made it easier. He looked to the left and to the right at the deserted courtyard. He smiled and spoke to him, soldier to soldier, "I can do better than that. If you would lend me your sword, we could spar for a few minutes."

Anthony turned his sword, pommel first, over to Mishimar without hesitation. Mishimar took a few practice swings with it while Anthony drew Hane, handed the scabbard to Hannah, and took his own few swings. The blade sang softly, which Mishimar noted as unusual. A singing sword should only sing for its owner. Perhaps something had been omitted from the legends. The smile of wonder on Anthony' face nearly brought tears to all their eyes.

"How good are you?" Mishimar asked sincerely.

Marcus' smile broadened, "I think I just got a whole lot better."

An exceptional centurion, Anthony led by example rather than only by command. That he fought alongside his men became quickly apparent. Mishimar was certainly glad he had been sparring nearly every night these past weeks with Hannah, because in Anthony' hands Hane had definitely come alive. While not an actual battle, their sparring session was as wondrous to hear as it was to behold. Fortunately Hane's song absorbed the normal clanging of sparing, and at a subdued volume, otherwise the beauty of it would have woken the entire palace. They fought probably longer than either of them had initially planned, because of the wonder. They finally stopped, both panting deeply and sweating heavily. Anthony reluctantly reached out to Hannah for the scabbard and re-sheathed Hane. Mishimar handed him back his sword in exchange for Hane.

"I can see why it was so difficult to part with such a weapon. I wish I had the time to hear its story, but I must return to my post." Anthony stepped forward, the two clasped forearms in the Roman fashion, and before he realized it, Mishimar had pulled him into an embrace.

"It has been a true pleasure to meet you, Anthony." Then his tone turned reverent. "The fact that my sword, Hane, sang in your hand is of special note." He smiled at the pun he had just made, and continued. "A singing sword usually only sings for its rightful owner, not that you ever truly own a singing sword. That he sang for you may very well mean that the two of you may meet again."

Anthony fumbled for words, probably a new experience for him, but he recovered. "Thank you for those words and the opportunity to...." He was again tongue-tied with emotion, as he looked longingly again at the sword, "to...spar with him."

"You are most definitely welcome," as he tied Hane back on. "I hope we shall meet again."

Anthony saluted them all, "'Til then, may your God speed you on your quest to find the king." And he turned and strode energetically back to the palace.

Seph spoke up, "Mishimar, can you get us back to the inn from here?"

He chuckled, "I most certainly can," and off they went.

Once in their suites, they went to their individual rooms, washrooms, and prepared for bed. They had agreed to meet in the dining room for a few minutes of debriefing before retiring, but when they assembled, their favorite old man had arrived before them.

∽

Seph began, "Uriel, were you there for all of that?"

Uriel smiled. He was much easier to talk to when he appeared as a man rather then when with wings and all he towered above you. "Yes, I was there and Eleazar is correct. We will leave for Bethlehem in the morning."

"And we will be looking for?" Seph asked.

Uriel continued, "A young boy not quite two years old, staying there with his mother and father. All three of these individuals are unique and special beyond your imagining."

Hannah interjected, "And the stories about his being born in a stable? That seems a strange way for the king of the Jews to enter the world."

"Ah yes, my friend Gabriel has been a part of all that, from the boy's conception, their travels from Nazareth, his birth, all the way until now. The Promised One has entered the world incognito and is living an unobtrusive life, much like you and your travels. But be assured, he is the one, the Promised One of old. As his father was told, 'And you shall name him Jeshua for he will save his people from their sins.' That is his destiny."

Chokmah finally found a voice, "And our part in all of this?"

"Ah, I think you can trust Chayeem to continue to guide you as He has until now. And, of course, I will be with you whether you can see me or not. Oh, and your inquires after the king in Bethlehem, they need to be discreet." Uriel stood up and Mishimar with him.

Hesitantly he asked, "Uriel, are you an angel or a star?"

Uriel smiled characteristically, "That is an interesting question, Mishimar. If you took a nearly unimaginably, powerful, and potentially destructive force and spun it into a sphere, you would have a star. Standing here with you, you have a person who can change from a frightening eight-cubit-tall being, complete with a singing sword," and he winked, "into a mild mannered old man," his smile broadened, "in the blink of an eye. What would you think?"

Lowering his head Mishimar responded, "I don't know, that's why I asked the question."

Uriel continued, "Let me ask you a question in return. Can you be a warrior against evil and also a lover of Hannah?"

Mishimar looked at Hannah and blushed.

"There, I think you have my answer." and he disappeared.

Mishimar sat back down, still blushing. The three Masters pushed back their chairs, stood, and excused themselves. Hannah remained seated, still a bit shocked.

"You love me?" Hannah ventured. Mishimar nodded his head silently up and down, watching her carefully. "When were you going to tell me?"

Sheepishly he answered, "I was afraid to believe it until this very moment."

"Hmm," she nearly sang, "this is like the first time you meet Chayeem. Even though it's happening, you're not entirely sure that it really is happening." she knelt down so she could look up into his downcast eyes.

"And you?" he ventured.

She reached out, took his sword hand, brought it to her lips, and replied, "I think I could say, I at least love this hand."

He looked back into her eyes as his heart filled. He knew she meant much more than that.

# Chapter 19
# The Second Charge

The next morning, after the travelers from the East had departed, Herod called Nebo to him while he finished his breakfast. The king sat at a table lavishly supplied with prepared food from all over the country, along with many fresh fruits and vegetables.

Nebo entered and stood across from the king's table. "You called me, your Majesty?"

The king looked up, his mouth still full, and mumbled, "Yes, what did you think about the events of last night and this new king?"

A malevolent smile began to spread across Nebo's face. "This confirms what my god has been telling me about a very real threat to your throne."

Herod picked up a sliver of wood and began picking his teeth. "But he's only a child. Do we need to worry about him now?"

"My Lord," Nebo continued, "It is easiest to pull a weed, before it has time to establish roots."

Herod put the sliver down and gave Nebo his full attention. "And how would you propose that we do that?"

Nebo's smile spread more, "Leave it to me, your Majesty. I will take care of it for you."

Herod smiled as well, "What did I ever do without you, Nebo?"

"It doesn't matter, you have me now, your Majesty."

"Yes, yes," he acknowledged, "I do indeed. Well, just take care of it. Use whatever resources you need. How many men will you require?"

"Thank you, my Lord, but I will require no men. I will handle this clandestinely." Nebo turned and left the king's presence. Herod returned to his breakfast with renewed vigor.

Nebo went to his chambers to wait for the return of his son. While he waited, he went into his study and recovered an ancient spell book that he had been given as a young man, from its secure hiding place. If anyone knew that this book was worth all the gold in the kingdom, they would ransack his place to find it, but they would not find it. Its hiding place was obscured with its own spells of concealment. Though not invisible, it might as well have been, for when you looked at it your attention immediately wandered. Nebo often wondered if the spell would also work on a person, but when he had tried it on a small kitten, the kitten could not see where it was and had wandered in a circle until it had dropped from exhaustion. Even though the cat was right at his feet, Nebo couldn't see it either until the spell broke when the cat lost consciousness. He would have to find a way to protect the next subject he tried it on. He spent the rest of the day pouring over the book in a vain attempt to find something to aid them on this current assignment. When Nesher came home, their servant girl, Zerah, had supper ready for them. After she had told the king about Nebo, the king had rewarded her by sending her to serve Nebo and his son. She cooked, washed, kept their house, and tried to anticipate their needs. She became virtually indispensable or maybe, because of her industriousness, they found that they required no other servants.

Nesher patted Zerah rather familiarly as she served them their dinner. "Another day guarding the king. It would be pretty boring if there were not something to look forward to." He winked at Zerah as she served his father.

"I'm afraid you will have to finish your evening activities quickly and get some early rest," Nebo said to his son. "I will need you to meet me in my underground temple at midnight tonight."

Nesher thought his original evening plans contained more alure. "You have something special planned?" That might be one option. "Or a new sparing partner for me?" That would be preferable.

"Something special," Nebo answered, "not a new partner. Marduk would like to meet with us."

Zarah looked at Nesher warily. Somethings about her new service she considered an improvement. Nesher was extremely fit, very good to look at and seemed genuinely pleased at her service. However, other conditions had not improved. While serving a volatile and violent king, had been like daily walking a fraying tightrope above a pit of alligators, Nebo and his relationship with the god Marduk frightened her beyond measure. She quickly disappeared into the kitchen.

Nesher watched her depart longingly, "Do you know what Marduk wants?"

"I believe it has something to do with the new king business of last night."

Nesher's eyes widened, "Are you thinking we may need to align ourselves with him while he is still a child?"

"I'm not sure what he wants, we'll have to wait and see." The rest of the meal passed with inconsequential small talk.

∽

Later, at midnight, Nesher met his father in the temple, in the room with its black altar. On the altar stood a small sacrificial bowl, usually containing the blood of some animal. At least it was not him on the altar. Nebo touched his staff to the bowl and the contents ignited, spewing a rather pungent smoke. As the smoke filled the room, Nebo continue to mutter some unintelligible incantations. When he finished, the smoke cleared to reveal a being of indescribable beauty. Nebo took one knee before him and Nesher followed suit.

"You require us, my Lord?" Nebo ventured.

The Being spoke with a melodic, but somewhat discordant voice, "Yes, I believe the king was visited by some men from the East last night, one carrying a wondrous sword."

"Yes, my Lord, they search for a child that they say will become king," Nebo responded.

"King, bah! Imposter is more like it." His song almost hurt their ears. "The child needs to be destroyed."

"You have but to tell us where he is, Lord, and we will make it happen," Nebo confidently interjected.

"I don't know where he is!" he spat out, "It is beyond even my vision."

"They said that they were following a star and that it would lead them to him." Nebo repeated what he had heard.

"They follow no star!" Marduk roared. "Did you idiots believe their foolish rantings?"

"What would you have us do, my Lord?" This was not going very well.

"Where were they headed?" Marduk hissed.

"The Hebrew priest, Eleazar, quoted from their ancient scriptures, a prophecy that said the new king would be born in Bethlehem. They will be going there," Nebo reported.

"Bethlehem, Bethlehem, Bethlehem," It was almost a chant. "Yes, that makes sense. Go to Bethlehem! Make a camp in the hills and set up your base of operations there. Have your spies watch the men from the East and when they find the imposter, report back to you. I will have my spies looking too. Then we will attack and destroy him." Glee returned to his voice. "Yes, this may very well work! Nesher, take the sword, Balak, with you! Go quickly, there isn't much time!" The panel to the sparring chamber opened and the Being vanished leaving behind the stench of burning flesh.

"Nesher," Nebo said firmly, "grab the sword. We must pack quickly and be on our way within the hour. There is no time to spare." Nesher stepped over to the table and grasped the scabbard, feeling once again the incredible power of this weapon. He felt invincible.

# Chapter 20
# One Final Inn

The day started long and kept getting longer. Wandering about a town discreetly asking everybody if they knew where the king was staying would be difficult, but over lunch they had developed a plan. Bethlehem is only about 48 stadia from Jerusalem, so packing up after breakfast and traveling that short distance had been fairly easy. It did take them some time to find an inn that could meet their needs since no one would consider Bethlehem a fascinating place to visit. They finally settled on renting a homestead on the outskirts of the city that had enough bedrooms and its own stable. They rented it for the week, not knowing how long their business would take. Hannah had the easiest time making discreet inquiries. Lots of news passed between women at the wells and in the marketplaces. Mishimar and Seph left in one direction to visit various inns and merchants throughout the city, while Chok and Raz left in the other direction.

Seph dressed a bit more prosperous-looking than usual and even brought a satchel of cloth samples with him. He had often wondered why he had been prompted to bring them on the trip. Mishimar simply acted as his bodyguard. They sincerely hoped no one would attempt to rob them. Once Mishimar's singing sword was let out of its sheath, the cat would be out of the bag.

Although Seph was not much of a drinker, he was glad he held his liquor well, as most of the well-to-do merchants they visited expected to discuss things over wine. They did not expect Mishimar to imbibe with them, thankfully. He needed all of his wits about him. The sign on this current establishment read, "Asher's Fine Textiles." A small bell tinkled as they entered.

A rather stylishly dressed young woman met them. "How may I help you?" She asked.

Seph smiled. He did have a wonderfully disarming smile. "I would like to see your proprietor, if he's in."

Her smile equaled his, "Yes.... SHE is in, may I ask who's calling?"

He took a gold coin out of his pocket, reached into his satchel, removed a small square of silk which he wrapped around the coin, and handed it to her. "I am Sepheth, a cloth merchant," he chuckled as though it hardly described him, "from the royal courts of the East. I am looking to expand my distribution network. Please take this gift to your mistress."

She took his hand in both of hers and before taking the package, she held his hand a little longer than expected, looking at the fine needlework of his sleeve. As she let go of his hand, she gazed back up into his eyes and hers somehow sparkled. "Yes, Sir, I'll tell her."

If they thought the clerk was well dressed, her mistress could have been a queen. Her gown was exquisite in every aspect: material, cut, embroidery work, buttons and clasps, accents, and it all fit her form and countenance exactly. It had been obviously made for her and her alone. Its effect left both men stunned. Seph fought the urge to kneel as she walked toward him and stretched out her hand. He took her hand and brought it to his lips as he bowed over it. Wanting to exclaim, "Your majesty....."

What he did say, when his breath returned, was, "Madame, this is an extreme pleasure. I am Sepheth, but I would be privileged if you called me Seph."

He found her smile as breath-taking as her gown, "And I am Abigail. I believe you have met my daughter, Miriam."

That explained why the young woman dressed and acted better than the usual clerk. "Yes we have." He bowed towards her also.

Abigail looked him straight in the eyes, "And while you are dressed very nicely, Seph, you are definitely not a cloth merchant, but most certainly well educated?"

Seph lowered his head, their ruse made him uncomfortable. "Ah, yes, I am sorry for that. We are trying to make some discreet inquires and it is difficult to do that as ourselves. I am afraid I am not particularly adept at deception or acting."

Still smiling, "Oh, you would have fooled most, but not me, I am afraid."

Something about this woman disconcerted him, "Again, I apologize for the ruse."

She reached out and took his hand, "Come into my parlor and we can talk privately." Seph actually blushed when she touched him. "Your bodyguard," and she winked at Mishimar "may keep my daughter company." Now it was Mishimar's turn to feel uncomfortable. Miriam made a hand gesture towards the sitting room and led the way.

"Would you like some tea?" Abigail already had a pot, covered in a warming blanket, and some delicate, fine china cups and saucers sitting on an ornately carved table between two large piles of velvet cushions. He nodded and she gestured for him to sit while she poured the tea. However, he waited until she handed him his tea and was seating herself before he sat as well.

"Now, to your discreet inquiries." Each time she smiled he felt as if the sun was breaking through the lone cloud in a deep blue otherwise cloudless sky.

"We do come from the East," he began, "that much is true." He felt as though he could tell her everything as he looked off to the left. There on the wall hung the most realistic painting of a large tree in the middle of a wondrous garden. On a plaque underneath it, engraved in Hebrew, he read the single word, "Chayeem." He gasped audibly and she chuckled lightly, like the tinkling of a small silver bell.

"Ah, I think you just discovered my secret," she said still chuckling.

Was this woman always going to catch him off guard? "You know Chayeem?"

"Yes," The sun still shone. "For most of my life."

Now he knew why he could speak freely. "He has sent us here, looking for the Promised One. We met his star in the East and he has guided us here."

"Ah, that would be Uriel, the one who covered the garden after the rebellion."

"You know Uriel too?" Who on earth was this woman? She did not answer his question directly, perhaps her own ruse.

"The child that you seek and his mother are staying at a small house on the outskirts of town." She spoke of them so easily. "The child was born here, in Bethlehem, almost two years ago. His stepfather runs a small carpenter's shop on the back of the house."

"Stepfather, his stepfather? She's divorced and remarried?" Something did not quite add up here.

"No." She said simply."This is her first marriage, but the carpenter is not his father."

Incredulity washed over Seph. "He's illegitimate?"

"You'll need to discuss that with them. I could send a message to them to expect you after supper."

He would not have thought he could be further amazed, "You know them that well?"

He was in danger of getting sunburned by her smile. "I'll just say, yes. Would you like me to do that for you?"

"Please," he stammered, finished his tea in a large swallow, and then thought it might have been rude, but Abigail seemed unfazed. She simply stood, offered her hand back to him, and let him walk with her back to the door. Miriam and Mishimar met them on the way.

Seph bowed and thanked her profusely, which she simply accepted graciously like everything else she did. After he and Mishimar had walked about one hundred cubits from the house Seph broke the silence. "Was Miriam as captivating as Abigail? Oh, I forgot, you are already in love." Seph continued to look at him wide-eyed. "That whole experience defied words!"

⟨∕⟩

The rest of the troupe was seated at dinner when Seph and Mishimar arrived. During their discreet inquires the others had uncovered bits and pieces of information about a new family which lived on the outskirts of town. They had lived there about two years and the husband was making quite a name for himself as a carpenter. They had a young boy, they kept pretty much to themselves, and there the gossip ended. Then came Seph and Mishimar's turn. Everyone else sat mesmerized as Seph described their time with Abigail and Miriam, from how she quickly saw through their disguise, all the way up to offering to send the family a message. "She said she would tell them to expect us tonight after supper."

They all joined in with something like, "Well that doesn't give us much time to get ready!" and jumped up from the table. Mishimar helped Hannah with the dishes, "You wash and I'll dry?" He asked. They were spending more time together as their romance blossomed. She left him to finish drying so she could make her own preparations to meet the child-king.

Mishimar still wore his best clean clothes. That would have to do. At least he had a singing sword to wear.

# Chapter 21
# A Simple Home

Mary and Joseph had truly enjoyed these last two years. Because of the scandal surrounding Jeshua's birth, she could not hide her pregnancy, they married in a small ceremony. Then came the census and the difficult journey to Bethlehem. They almost had not made it in time for his birth. What had been even harder to bear was the rejection. In a town full of people, many whom were their relatives, no one would show them hospitality, even with her advanced pregnancy. If not for an empathetic inn keeper and his wife, they probably would have had to deliver him out in the fields or worse. As it was, Mary gave birth in a stable and the baby was laid in a cattle trough. At least they kept him warm and dry there, amongst all the animals. The delivery seemed easy for a first child. The innkeeper's wife had acted as midwife and they had slept fairly well until some shepherds showed up with stories of angelic appearances and proclamations: "For unto you this night in the city of David, a savior has been born, the anointed of the Lord." They called him savior and worshipped him. Later followed the prophecies at his circumcision and dedication.

A man named Simeon had said, "And a sword will pierce your own soul..."

"*What in heaven's name did that mean?*" she thought.

Anna, who went to the temple daily, gave thanks to God and spoke to all who were waiting for the redemption of Israel about their son. They returned to Nazareth, but found such a cold  reception among their relatives that they returned to Bethlehem for these last two years.

Jeshua was taking his nap and Joseph had come in from his shop, "Do you suppose it will always be like this, Joseph?"

They felt lonely, but happy, "We are slowly beginning to be accepted here, I think."

"That is because your work is so wonderful, my husband." She admired him for the reputation he had built in such a short time. Those who had considered their son illegitimate had left and fortunately had kept their views mostly to themselves. But still, it took a lot of hard work to start a business in a new town. He had begun by making simple farm implements, but recently had completed some beautiful pieces of furniture. He now had a number of commissions waiting for him to find the time to complete them.

"Yes, even with our seemingly unfortunate beginning, it seems we are experiencing the favor of God." Although a humble man, he remained rightfully proud of his work and that his young wife had stuck with him through this rough patch of life. People were fickle. On the one hand they could be so cruel, even without true reason, but on the other hand perseverance and hard work could win them over.

They sat on a couch of cushions that he had built with his own hands, holding each other for a few more minutes. Then out of the bedroom walked their son, with a smile that brightened the heart of heaven. He came close to them, looked into their eyes, and said, "Momma, Papa, I just had good dream. Wonder is coming." He climbed up into their laps.

They both looked at each other and Joseph asked, "What is it, my son?" but he just snuggled into them and said no more. They shrugged their shoulders, sat together, and held one another for a few minutes until Joseph said, "I should go back out and work on that bench."

Jeshua asked, "I come, Papa?"

And Joseph smiled, "Yes, son you may come, too."

They got up, Joseph took Jeshua's hand, and together he and his father walked out to Joseph's workroom.

Mary could hear the sanding and occasionally Jeshua's giggling, while she began to prepare their evening meal. As the sun was going down, a message arrived from Abigail that they might have some visitors after supper. She wondered what that meant. She had met Abigail in the market and while she seemed very prosperous, she had never treated Mary in a condescending way. They had quickly become friends. Abigail had a very special way with people and everyone that met her spoke very warmly about her. Maybe she was sending Joseph some more business. Mary smiled. Abigail's recommendations greatly contributed to his current waiting list..

Mary called her boys, just as the sun was setting. They advanced on her, both smiling and covered in wood dust. She threw a towel at Joseph, "You shake off that dust and wash up before you come in my house," but she smiled too. They went back to the well, shook out their tunics and washed themselves off. Then hand in hand again they returned to the house. They ate a simple, but delicious meal. If more people sampled Mary's bread, her bread would be as famous as Joseph's carpentry. Before they sat, they joined hands, and Jeshua looked up at his father, who nodded. He looked up at the end of the table, "Thank you, Papa, for this," and his eyes looked around to take in the food, his parents, their home, "Amen." He let go of their hands and climbed on his cushion at the table. Joseph reclined beside him while Mary shook her head behind him. Jeshua had not spent much time in baby talk, but had proceeded quickly to full words and now simple sentences. She hoped his precociousness would continue to be a good thing. Maybe it would, but then again, maybe not.

After supper, when they had cleared off the table, Mary busied herself with the dishes, Jeshua looked up at his father and simply said, "We play blocks?" Joseph smiled, nodded, and Jeshua went to the corner, dragged out a box that was almost as large as himself, and pulled it over to the table. With each project Joseph completed he specially shaped some more blocks and added them to the box which now threatened to overflow. Jeshua looked at his father again and said, almost commandingly, "Towers!" Joseph smiled and gestured for Jeshua to go first. He stationed himself on the opposite side of the box, carefully selected a block, and set it on the table. The goal was to see who could build the tallest tower without it falling over. Jeshua showed ample skill at the game. He had good spatial ability, planned well, and best of all, he was patient. When Jeshua came to the point that he could no longer reach the top of his tower, Joseph signaled, him to wait a minute. He emptied the rest of the blocks on the floor, upturned the box so Jeshua could now stand on it, and added a few blocks on top of the box. Joseph wondered whether he should lose on purpose just to give his son confidence, but it did not look like he would need to this time. He had built his base wider than Jeshua's, but not by much and Joseph's tower teetered alarmingly. Jeshua carefully selected another block, climbed on the box, and placed it on the top of his tower. Mary walked in from the kitchen, wiping her hands on a dish towel, as Joseph placed his block on the top of his tower. A knock sounded at the door, startling Joseph, and his tower came crashing down. Jeshua smiled as Joseph just shook his head in defeat. Mary answered the door.

# Chapter 22
# The New King

Before they left for the house on the outskirts of the city, an old man joined them. "Uriel, you're coming with us?" Seph questioned.

"This is, I believe, why we came here, to meet the Promised One," he answered.

"So, you know then that Abigail has sent a message to them and that we are to be expected?" another question.

"Ah, so you met Abigail. She is really something. You know, she is one of us?" For an angel and an old man, he could be really exasperating sometimes.

"Abigail's an angel?" asked Hannah.

"I didn't say that, just that she is one of us." He obviously enjoyed the verbal sparring too much. "Come on, we'll be late," and he headed for the door.

"How are you going to get there?" She asked, but quickly regretted her question. He was an angel after all. She stepped through the doorway and almost fell over. Before her stood a majestic horse who made Mishimar's black stallion look like a common nag.

Uriel snickered and so did the horse, "I thought I would just ride with you."

Hannah reached out her hand to the horse's nose. He lowered his head, and he said "Ah, Hannah, I have heard much about you." Before she could even form the words in her mind, he added, "I am Gadol."

She stammered, "'Majesty,' that's fitting." She rubbed his nose as Uriel mounted him with unusual ease for the old man he appeared to be.

They all mounted and Seph said to Uriel, "We know the general direction, but you probably know the exact house?"

"Yes, I do," and Uriel led the way.

It did not take them long to ride through the town, the streets being pretty deserted for that time of night. The few people they did pass admired the old man and his horse. Some even waved in greeting. They had just entered the countryside when they came upon the small house. Light still came from the windows, so the message must have reached them in time. They dismounted and Hannah asked, "Should I stay with the horses?"

Uriel smiled, "I'm sure you can just ask them to wait for us. You do have Gadol with you, remember." She smiled in return and had a short word with the horses. Uriel stepped up, knocked on the door, and then stepped back. A young woman opened the door and it felt like meeting Abigail again. They fought the desire to fall to their knees. "*Who is this woman?*" they all asked themselves.

Then from behind her they heard, "Who is it, Momma?" The sound of his voice did drive them all to their knees, as the young child stepped to his mother's side and took her hand.

An older man stepped up behind them and said, "Welcome, please come into our home and be blessed."

As the three of them slowly got back up from their knees, the child disappeared with a, "Me Papa," only to return with a basin of water and a towel. As each one of them stood, stepped through the doorway, and announced themselves, the man and woman embraced them. Seph stepped through first.

"I am Seph," he said.

"I am Joseph," and he embraced him, "and this is my wife, Mary," and she embraced him. Then Seph stepped forward, removed his sandals, and Jeshua, who knelt at the basin, washed his feet. First the right, "Jeshua blesses you," he said and dried his foot. And then the left, "Welcome home." And after drying it he bent over and kissed it. The genuine tenderness struck them deeply.

The blessing repeated as each person entered and the simple welcoming, especially by the child, brought tears to each of their eyes. Second to last came Mishimar. When the child finished washing and drying Mishimar's left foot, he reached up and touched his sword's scabbard saying, "Hane, welcome home," then he bowed and kissed Mishimar's foot. How in heaven's name could this child know the name of his sword. Mishimar nearly wept outright.

Finally the old man stepped through the doorway. "I am Uriel, I have brought these people to meet you." After a moment of stunned silence, Joseph embraced him and then Mary embraced him. When Jeshua finished kissing Uriel's feet, Jeshua whispered, "I know you."

Uriel quickly put a finger to his lips and whispered back, "Our secret."

After they reclined around the table, with cups of water for each of them, and a plate of bread making the rounds. Seph asked the burning question. "How much does your son know about who he is?"

Mary looked at Joseph and he spoke. "We have shared some of the stories with him, but how much he believes is really true, I don't know. We know it's true and it's still difficult for us to believe. There were an awful lot of angels involved in all of this. An angel spoke to my wife, then later, one to me in a dream. An angel spoke to the shepherds and then a whole host of them sent the shepherds to us. But that was all years ago. Now we have begun to have a normal life and it's sort of wonderfully plain."

"Well," said Seph, "an angel brought us here," he looked at Uriel, "and now Herod knows about your son. So, I think normal and plain are about to be disrupted again." Addressing Mishimar and Hannah, "Could you bring in the packages we left with the horses?" They nodded and left. The rest of them continued with small talk about the last two years until Hannah and Mishimar returned. They gave each of the Masters the gift they had packed. Jeshua sat on Mary's lap. Seph stood with his package, walked around the table and knelt next to Mary and the boy.

He placed a small chest on the table and opened it to reveal the gold it contained. "This is to honor you, Jeshua, as the Promised One and our King," He bowed in worship.

Raz stepped from behind Seph and knelt, placing his box on the table, "And I bring frankincense to honor you." And he too bowed.

Then Chok came to kneel. "And I brought you myrrh, though I'm not sure why I was led to bring it as it is usually used for burial." He also bowed. During the time the three presented their gifts, the other three had slipped off their cushions to also kneel reverently.

Joseph stood, "I'm not sure how to respond to these lavish gifts, but I thank you for them and the honor you have bestowed upon my son."

Jeshua reached out, took one of the gold coins, admired it, put it back in the box, smiled, and said, "Thank you."

Joseph asked, "What will you do now?"

Seph responded, "Herod asked that we return to Jerusalem and tell him where you live, but that doesn't seem to make any sense. So we're not sure at this point. We will have to ask Chayeem about it."

Jeshua looked up quickly and said. "Chayeem, yes."

They all looked wonderingly at one another. The travelers stood and prepared to leave, embracing one another as they said their goodbyes. Once outside, the family stood in the doorway, framed in the light of the room behind them. It made a picture that would remain with the travelers for a long time. They began mounting their horses when Jeshua ran up to Mishimar, "Please, I see Hane?" and he pointed to the sword. Mishimar smiled and drew Hane from his sheath to sing a note so pure they each wanted to cry out with joy. He knelt and held the sword out to Jeshua on his palms.

Jeshua kissed his fingers and than ran them along the blade as he said, "Bless you, Hane," then looked Mishimar in the eyes, "you too." Then he ran back to join his parents. Mishimar sheathed the sword and mounted his stallion. As they rode off, they all turned, almost in unison, to wave at the family who stood waving back at them.

∽

That night they dreamt of all the wonders of what they had experienced. They had seen with their own eyes what righteous men and prophets for hundreds of years had desired to see. They had seen the Promised One. However, Mishimar dreamed differently. He saw himself saddling his horse then suddenly turning around, drawing Hane in the process. There stood Uriel in all of his terrible splendor, "Wake the others now! You must leave quickly. As you have already determined, do not go back to Jerusalem!" Mishimar found himself wide awake. He quickly rousted the others and got them on the road within an hour.

Raz asked Seph,"What about the money we paid for our lodgings? We paid for an entire week!"

Seph replied, "That will be part of our ruse. Because we paid for a full week, they will think we are just on a side trip and coming back." And they departed another way.

❦

Uriel also appeared to Joseph in his dreams, "Get up and flee to Egypt. Take Mary, the boy, and stay there until I tell you to return, for Herod is seeking for your son that he may destroy him." Early that next morning, they took the gifts the Masters had given them, and quickly packed. Joseph had to awaken the stable master, but through the favor of the Lord purchased four adequate horses. And so, the holy family fled towards Egypt.

# Chapter 23
# Ambushed

Because they traveled home by a different way and had completed their task, they felt they no longer had any need for concealment. They kept to the main road and they rode together. Mishimar led the way and Hannah brought up the rear as before. They still traveled with all their gear so they made slow progress, but they felt less encumbered.

Meanwhile, Marduk had led Herod's sorcerer, Nebo, and his son Nesher, with the sword Balak, to a place of concealment on a road leading from Bethlehem.

"Father, why has Marduk led us here? The travelers from the East would not take this road back to Jerusalem," ventured Nesher.

"He believes that the Masters have seen through Herod's subterfuge and will not return to Jerusalem to tell him where the child is staying," his father answered.

"But our spies followed them and already know where the child lives. Why don't we just go back and tell Herod?" he still questioned.

"I will return to Herod with that information," said Nebo rather curtly. "You should prove more than a match for their bodyguard, regardless of his weapon."

"Why do we care about these Masters, anyway?"

"Because no one defies the king without suffering the consequences. Do you understand?" The continued questions frustrated Nebo.

"Yes, Sir!" Nesher replied with mock submission. "I'll take care of them, all of them!"

∽

As the sun began to rise, the three Masters, Mishimar, and Hannah still rode rather casually, their mission to find the new king accomplished. They chatted with light hearts while Mishimar kept ahead, but within sight of the rest of them, although he felt no particular concern regarding their safety. Old habits just die with difficulty.

Suddenly he sensed something. He turned to see a mounted warrior charging at him from the right. Instead of completing the charge, he unexpectedly pulled up at the last second and in one fluid movement dismounted. Mishimar stayed mounted, noting that this potential foe had oddly given up both his advantage of surprise and being mounted.

"I am here to frustrate the completion of your quest!" Nesher challenged.

"You're too late, we have already completed it." Mishimar responded.

"But the king ordered you to return to him with news of where the new king was, did he not?" His challenge continued.

"Herod is not our king, he does not command us!" Mishimar stated matter-of-factly as he too dismounted. The Masters and Hannah moved their horses back, huddled together, and wondered what kind of a crazy duel might ensue. Then Hannah too dismounted, though the Masters tried to prevent her.

∽

Nesher, having discarded the place of his father's concealment to initiate his charge and then his challenge, pulled Balak from its sheath, the pommel with no visible blade. Mishimar responded by pulling Hane from his own to crack the morning air with a note of purest beauty. Time slowed and nearly stopped as they stood facing each other.

They slowly began to circle each other, trying to gauge one another's strengths and weaknesses from what they observed, their posture, their walk, how they handled their swords, the attention to detail in the way they dressed, but most importantly what they saw in each other's eyes.

Nesher was clothed almost royally. His body armor was made of the finest leather and cut to fit him perfectly. A heavily ornamented, golden armlet graced his right forearm, a blood red ruby ring on his left hand. His long hair was tied back with an embroidered band about his forehead, complete with sacred signs and occult symbols. The plain bronze armlet on his left forearm was obviously more functional than ornamental.

Mishimar, on the other hand, was the picture of simplicity. He had no adorning trinkets, just a loose homespun tunic, covering plain leather breeches. His only costly apparel were his travel boots, which while well made were also well worn.

Nesher's eyes were a haughty, confident, steel grey, devoid of emotion which stared with an air of condescension. Mishimar's eyes were a warm brown, belying a settled peace. He was obviously comfortable with himself, yet filled with a deep passion that simmered just below the surface.

∽

Time snapped back into full speed, as they both lept into action. The sound of their battle rang with hope and despair. Hane sang brightly, brilliantly, while Balak sought to nullify and suck the life out of each note. Their dance was both beautiful and terrible to behold, as light and dark embrace, each desperately seeking the upper hand. Neither seemed able to create an advantage; they were too evenly matched. They broke, took a step back, both panting heavily.

Nesher threw something at Mishimar's head with his left hand accompanied by a word of mumbled incantation. Mishimar blocked the projectile with his left hand and it seemed to drop harmlessly to the ground, but for a moment his vision was confused and befuddled. He seemed to quickly recover and they engaged again, but something seemed wrong. Mishimar whispered between breaths, "Chayeem?" and heard a resounding, "I am here!" in his heart. Everything instantaneously cleared and his strength renewed. Mishimar began to gauge the rhythm of Nesher's battling. He feinted a fault that should have allowed him to disarm Nesher, when from seemingly nowhere, a small animal, startled by the conflict, bolted across the path of Mishimar and Nesher. For just a moment Mishimar was distracted, concerned for the animal, and in that moment Nesher altered his grip, smashed Mishimar on the side of the head and knocked him unconscious, his sword clattering to the ground. The battle seemed won, yet Hannah ran towards the still form of Mishimar. .

∽

Nesher stepped over Mishimar's body before she was fully there, "Pick up and give me his sword and I will spare his life." he gloated.

Hannah slowly reached down, picked up Mishimar's sword, and before Nesher could dispatch Mishimar as he had planned, she launched her own attack on Nesher. Through clenched teeth she muttered, "You've lost your advantage?"

Suddenly a portal opened, a circle of light filled with darkness and in its middle the luminescent one, Marduk, as he was currently called, with his sword drawn. "No, I am his advantage!"

Yet at the same moment Uriel appeared, at his full height, and with his sword drawn. "No! You are not!"

They all joined in battle, Hannah against Nesher, Marduk against Uriel. Thus the battle of the four singing swords began. The cataclysmic nature of this conflict soon had the very air humming, the ground vibrating, as they clashed in attack, parry, counter-attack; blow after blow after blow. Hannah attacked Nesher with such ferocity that he was forced back, left breathless, unable to think of, let alone utter any incantations. Mentally, physically, spiritually exhausted he faltered, and she seeing the advantage slayed him. She turned to aid Uriel in his battle with Marduk. Marduk noticed her turning towards him in his peripheral vision and after a quick parry of Uriel's attack, stepped back and stopped.

Marduk muttered, "I have frustrated your attempt to protect the child! You and the woman are no match for me!"

Uriel laughed, "Would you like me to call for reinforcements? Only one third of the angels followed you in your rebellion. The other two thirds would love to join me."

Marduk commanded, "That sword belonged to one of my angels." Pointing to the spot where Nesher's sword lay, only its pommel visible. He extended his hand, towards it. "Give it to me!"

Uriel looked to Hannah, "No! By right of combat, she has earned it"

Marduk sneered, "Then, by right of combat, give me his," pointing to Mishimar's sword that Hannah held.

Mishimar had started to regain consciousness.

"Hmmm..." Uriel's smile returned, "It doesn't appear

that Nesher won the right to that sword either. Mishimar is still alive!"

Marduk discarded his battle stance, sheathed his sword, and spat out, "Then I will return at a more opportune moment." the dark portal reappeared and he stepped back through it.

Hannah moved back to Mishimar, knelt, scooped his head and shoulders into her arms. His eyes fluttered open and he looked into hers. There was silence for a moment and then he whispered, "Is this heaven?" She smiled, leaned her face close to his and kissed him full on the lips. She whispered back, "Maybe..." He sat slowly up shaking his head, unsure what had just happened. Just to make sure he was back in reality, he reached up, pulled her back down to him, and kissed her. After a moment, she pushed him away gently and handed him his sword. She walked over, picked up Nesher's discarded sword by the hilt, and suddenly saw the blade of Balak. She rolled over Nesher's body with her foot, reached down and removed the sword's scabbard. She took it for herself and sheathed the sword in it. She returned to Mishimar, extended her hand, and pulled him up to his feet.

∽

Uriel, Hannah, and Mishimar turned to face the three Masters. At some time during the battle they too had dismounted and stood there with their mouths wide open in amazement.

Finally Seph muttered, barely above a whisper, "What have we just witnessed?"

Uriel replied calmly, "The child and his family have fled Bethlehem, in a direction of which the enemy is unaware. He wanted to eliminate us before they went back and eliminated them, but I have warned Jeshua's parents."

Seph continued, "Warned them of what?"

"That they needed to flee to Egypt for Herod will seek

to destroy the threat to his throne."

Chok finally found his voice, "And what now?"

"I think it will be safe for you to return home. You are in no more immediate danger," said Uriel.

Chok spoke again, "And what about the three of you?"

Uriel looked at Mishimar and Hannah, "I can't speak for them, but I will join myself to the child and his family. Every one of the Lord's little ones needs a guardian angel." And he disappeared.

Raz also looked at the couple, "And you two?"

Maishimar looked at Hannah and she nodded in agreement. "I think we will follow Uriel a while longer."

Seph raised his hand skyward, "Then the peace of Chayeem be upon us all, as we travel our separate ways." The two groups came together and embraced one another, last of all Seph and Hannah. As they broke their embrace, she reached out and touched his cheek.

"Goodbye, 'Other Father,' may the time between us be short."

With either a twinkle or a tear in his eye he responded, pointing to Mishimar, "Take good care of her, you have my blessing." Mishimar and Hannah raised their singing swords to them in a salute, turned, and rode off in the other direction, hoping to intercept the holy family as they fled to Egypt.

The Masters mounted up, turned their horses towards the East, and began their journey home.

# Chapter 24
# Back in Jerusalem

Nebo usually had no difficulty seeing the king. In fact sometimes he thought his place as the king's most trusted wizard and sorcerer so secure that he could just come and go as he pleased. For some reason, today the guard refused him entrance. Even his hidden access door seemed locked and he did not think anyone else even knew the secret door existed.

He returned again and again, telling the guard, "It is urgent I see the king."

And continued to be rejected with, "He is with someone and asked that he not be disturbed under any circumstance."

Finally Nebo added, "But what if it concerns the security of his throne and a plot to overthrow him?"

But the guard just shook his head, "I'm sorry Nebo, but I have my orders."

In desperation, he pulled a chair from the antechamber, placed it near the door, sat in it and said, "I'll wait, but I must see him immediately. As soon as he is available."

The guard thought, "This must really be important, I have never seen Nebo miss a meal, as he sat there all through lunch, until he fell asleep in the chair." Finally, the door opened and startled Nebo awake. Out stepped a woman of exquisite beauty and smelling so powerfully of witchcraft that he nearly fainted.

She walked up to him and whispered, "Nebo, we've been expecting you. You may come with me." She held out her hand. Before he realized what he was doing, she led him into the king's throne room. The door to the king's personal chambers stood open. It too smelled powerfully of witchcraft.

The king sat on his throne a vacant look in his eyes and he was smiling naively. "Ah, Nebo, and what can we do for you? I see you have met Batel."

"My Lord," he stammered. This woman's intoxicating presence nearly had the better of him. "I'm returning from Bethlehem. The Masters are not coming back to report on the whereabouts of the new king, but my spies have located him."

"Good, good. Guard!" he shouted. His guard stuck his head in and the king commanded, "Call Anthony and have him attend me." The guard left to comply.

A chair had been placed at the king's right hand and Batel sat in it and held the king's hand. "I was wondering if it was time I took another wife." He looked up at her numbly.

"My King, it would be against my vows to marry, I am betrothed to Chemosh, but that shouldn't get in the way of our enjoying each other's company." And she actually winked at him.

Anthony walked in. He had barely washed the dust from his hands and face and tiredness hung on his shoulders like a cloak. "My Lord?" and he took one knee. Batel's eyes brightened considerably, but Anthony still had his head bowed. He looked wearily in Nebo's direction. "Nebo." He stalled trying to find the words. "I have some bad news. One of my patrols found your son slain on a road out of Bethlehem to the East. I went to investigate and it appears he was alone, but defended himself well from a number of attackers. I'm not sure why they attacked him. All they took was his sword and left him where he was slain."

Anthony might as well have cold-cocked him. Nebo sat stunned. Before grief had a moment to set in, the king sat up straighter on his throne and said, "Anthony, Nebo has located this new king that has been born." He continued, "Nebo, show him." Somehow Nebo shook off the news for the moment.

Off to the left stood a table where the king sometimes dined when he and his generals strategized for battle. Nebo stepped to the table and reached inside of his robe. Weary as he was, Anthony had his sword halfway drawn before Nebo could get his hand back out of his robe to show the map he had brought with him. Anthony relaxed. Nebo spread the map of Bethlehem and its surrounding countryside on the table.

"My spies said he is located here," as he pointed to the map. "It's a small house on the outskirts of town without defenses. It should be easy to capture him."

"Capture him?" the King raised his voice. "I don't want him captured. Kill him."

Suddenly the weariness fell off of Anthony as if he had simply removed a cloak. "But sire, he is just a child, he poses no threat."

"No threat?" Herod abruptly stood. He looked back at Batel and she nodded. "This is a child of prophecy, born of religion, and you say he is not a threat?"

"A simple peasant child, my Lord." He tried again.

"Was he involved in the murder of Nebo's son? Are his followers already beginning their attack on my throne? No! This stops here and it stops now!" He had built up quite a head of steam. Perhaps he was trying to impress Batel. "Don't only kill him, kill every male child two years old and younger."

Anthony was appalled. "But my King."

"Nesher has already failed us and died for it. Who else must die? This threat must be cleansed from my land. Go quickly, do it now!" He sounded nearly hysterical.

With a heavy heart, Anthony bowed, and turned to Nebo on his way to comply. "Nebo, my men have brought your son's body to your chambers. I am sorry for your loss." He left the king's presence to accomplish the most difficult command of his life. He assembled his troops, gave them their orders, and they dared not question them. They had just brought home one slain in battle and now they must be the bringers of death to the innocent. They could tell how this had affected their commander and dared not add to that sorrow.

Nebo dragged his son's body down to his underground temple, lay him on the black altar, doused him in oil and lit him afire. In anguish he cried out, "Marduk, you have taken everything from me!" Then he too stepped into the flames.

# Epilogue

Because they began their journey early in the morning and rode on horses this time, they kept ahead of most travelers and met few others on the road. Jeshua rode in front of his father, almost on his lap. He thought this quite an adventure and seemingly had not picked up on any of the danger Mary and Joseph felt at all. Mary rode beside Joseph and they almost took turns looking back to see if their pursuers had caught up. Amidst feeling a sense of haste, they still had the presence of mind to realize that an occasional rest period would allow them to travel further and faster if they stayed refreshed. They stopped a number of times along their way and then in one of the villages. They cleaned up and had lunch at a small wayside inn.

Fortunately Joseph had enough change left over from the purchase of the horses that he did not need to use any more of their gold. He tried to be careful not to bring undue attention to them, but maintain the appearances of a simple traveling craftsman and his family, relocating. He had barely enough time to gather his carpenter's tools before they left, but he had been able to bring the most important ones. As they finished their meal, Jeshua turned to the doorway and announced, "Uriel." Sure enough the old man walked through the doorway, came over, sat down and joined them.

He said softly enough that only they could hear him, "When you stop for the evening, rent an extra room. Mishimar and Hannah should be joining us by then."

"Only one room?" Joseph raised an eyebrow.

"She and Mary can stay in one, you, Mishimar, and the boy in the other." he said matter of factly.

"You stay?" asked Jeshua.

Uriel looked at him and smiled, "I am always here with you, you just can't always see me."

Jeshua smiled in return and nodded his head confidently.

⸎

At that evening's inn they were fortunate enough to rent the two rooms separated by their own sitting room. After supper, they were sitting there when Hannah and Mishimar knocked on their door. Joseph let them in. They had a warm and cozy fire going in the fireplace.

Joseph asked them, "Have you eaten?"

Mishimar responded, "Yes, when Uriel confirmed that you were indeed at this inn, we had supper downstairs before we came up."

Joseph continued, "He is rather helpful isn't he. He told us you were coming and to rent a second room."

Mishimar looked at Hannah as she raised an eyebrow, but Joseph went on, "So Hannah, you and Mary will have one room and the guys the other." Hannah sighed noticeably in relief.

"You have probably already figured out that we would like to accompany you to Egypt. Did Uriel mention that too?" Mishimar calmly added.

"No, he just said you were meeting us here." But Joseph was smiling, he had taken Jeshua onto his lap.

Mishimar drew his sword, the room filling with its music. He knelt on one knee, with the sword across his palms. Hannah did the same, although her sword, with its invisible blade, sang nothing.

Mishimar began, "Jeshua, I would like to pledge my life and my sword to you for as long as you need them." Although Jeshua had already blessed Hane, he slipped off his father's lap, once again kissed his fingers, touched the blade, and said, "Yes."

Likewise, Hannah presented Balak, pommel in one palm and the other palm under its invisible blade, "I too pledge my life and this sword to you for as long as you need us."

Jeshua surprisingly responded, "No!" Then he reached out, wrapped his fingers around the invisible blade, and said, "Be, Oz!" and the shimmering blade became visible and its song filled the room in harmony with Hane's.

Uriel also became visible and said, "He will make all things new, some by restoring them to their original newness. That sword was Oz, which means Glory, before the beginning of time."

Jeshua said, "Now, yes!"

The entire extended family smiled and basked in the sacred moment for just a bit longer, until Uriel said, "Good night." and disappeared.

Mishimar laughed, "Is he always going to be doing that?" and the rest of the family joined in his laughter.

The next morning they found Jeshua kneeling out on the balcony of their suite, eyes closed, facing the sun as it rose over the hills, smiling, and humming a catchy little tune. Joseph squatted next to him, reached out, and lightly put his arm around his shoulder. "What are you humming?" he whispered to him.

Jeshua opened his large brown eyes, "Sing Papa song." He announced proudly, looking out into the sky.

Joseph smiled too, "Come have breakfast with us."

"Okay." and he hopped up to his feet rather agilely for a two year old, took Joseph's hand, and they walked back into the sitting room.

Hannah and Mishimar had returned from downstairs with bowls of warm mash and fresh water. The five of them reclined with their bowls as Jeshua said, "Uriel pray?"

The old man appeared, looked heavenward, "You are God of the heavens and the earth, of all that has life. Thank You for this provision, as we follow You to Egypt."

They all said, "Amen." Mishimar filled cups, passed them around, and they all ate heartily.

As they were finishing their meal, Hannah said to Jeshua, "Do you want to help with dishes?"

"Yup." was his simple reply as he stood and began to collect bowls and cups with her.

While the rest packed up their meager belongings, Hannah filled two basins, normally used for bathing, with water. One for washing, one for rinsing, as Jeshua picked up a towel, looked at Mishimar, smiled, and asked her, "Me dry?"

She nodded, "Normally, at an Inn, people just leave dirty dishes, but we like to show people that we value them and their possessions. So, we wash our dishes."

Standing a little taller, Jeshua added, "and dry, good." as he stacked them on the sideboard. When they were through, he handed her the towel to dry her hands, then dried his own, and hung the towel neatly where the morning sun would soon find it.

It was a cool crisp sunlit morning. The men had brought the horses, who each having had a good night's rest seemed eager for the next leg of their journey. Mishimar's horse, Shadow, seemed especially excited. Jeshua walked over to him, put a hand on his flank, then to his nose when he lowered his head. Shadow instantly quieted. Hannah looked at Mishimar and they both raise their eyebrows.

Jesuha also looked at Mishimar and exclaimed, "Ride, mister?"

Who looked questioningly to Joseph, "Is it okay if Jeshua rides with me this morning?"

Joseph shrugged, "If it's okay with you."

Mishimar mounted while Joseph helped Mary onto her horse and then he mounted his. Hannah handed Jeshua up to Mishimar and then she too mounted her horse.

Riding in front of Mishimar, Jeshua leaned forward to grasp his horse's neck. "Like Shadow, mister." He said over his shoulder. The horse whinnied and Mishimar asked himself, "*How does this child know the name of both my sword and my horse?*" Mary and Joseph also held the reigns of their pack horses, and off they all rode out of town. They were early enough again to be before most travelers. Once they were far enough away from the village, Hannah began to sing, Mishimar joined in, harmonizing, and Jeshua hummed along.

> *One day the One will come,*
> > *rising like the morning sun.*
> *One day a light will dawn,*
> > *making all things new.*
> *One day our wandering hearts,*
> > *lost, alone, and far from home*
> *One day we'll find Him close at hand.*
>
> *Light invading darkest night,*
> > *blindness giving way to sight*
> *Chaos calmed by peacefulness within.*
> *All our hopeless striving cease,*
> > *life is finding its release*
> *Death is swallowed up by life again.*
>
> *One day all of our despair,*
> > *all our pain and every care*
> *One day it will wash away and sin will be no*
> > *more,*

*One day we will all be home,*
　　　*finding that His kingdom's come*
*One day He will rule again,*
　　*as He has since time began.*

*One day, one day,*
　　　*we will see the Tree again*
*There will be an ending of all strife.*

*One day, one day, everything is new again*
*Drinking from the river of His life.*

# The End

Uriel

If you enjoyed this book, please head over to Amazon and write a review (scroll down until you see this book)! Your review helps an independent publisher tremendously, and I truly appreciate your time. Thank you!

# Glossary of Names

| | |
|---|---|
| Abigail | Owner of Asher's One Textiles in Bethlehem |
| Anna | Prophetess at Jeshua's dedication |
| Anthony | Herod's centurion |
| Antigonus | Last Maccabean king |
| Aristobulus | Mariamme's brother and High Priest |
| Avram | Seph's math tutor and instructor in Hebrew |
| Balak | Singing sword given to Ishbe-benob, then to Nesher |
| Batel | Herod's new witch |
| Beker | Hope's young camel |
| Chayeem | The Tree of Life in the Garden Delight's center |
| Chokmah (Chok) | Master of Religions |
| Choom | Halek's (Kel) horse |
| Clay | First man, caretaker of Delight |
| Daath | The Tree of Knowing good and evil |
| Dawn | First woman, co-caretaker with man (Clay) |
| Delight | God's wonderful garden |
| Eleazar | Scholar and priest in Herod's court |
| Gadol | Uriel's horse, Majesty |
| Halek | Kel's name as a wanderer |
| Halel | Conductor, choreographer of worship, covering angel of Delight who falls from his exalted position |
| Hane | Formerly Goliath's singing sword, Favor, now Mishimar's |
| Hannah | Seph's housekeeper |
| Herod Antipater | Herod the Great's father |

| | |
|---|---|
| Herod (the Great) | Current King of the Jews (Judea) |
| Hope | Daughter of Clay and Dawn |
| Jeruel | The sacrificial lamb, son of sheep Seh and Rachel |
| Joseph | Herod the Great's younger brother |
| Joseph | Jeshua's step-father |
| Kel | Clay's firstborn |
| Marduk | Nebo's god, the being of indescrib able light's other name |
| Mariamme | Herod's wife, granddaughter of the Maccabean Hyrcanus |
| Markus | Herod the Great's centurion |
| Mark Anthony | Emperor of Rome |
| Mary | Jeshua's mother |
| Matthan | Mishimar's grandfather |
| Midnight | Hannah's father's horse, Opelyeem |
| Miriam | Abigail's daughter, clerk at Asher's Fine Textiles |
| Mishimar | Soldier, with a singing sword, who accompanies Hannah and the Masters to Jerusalem |
| Nebo | Herod's wizard and master of the black arts |
| Nesher | Son of the wizard Nebo, possessor of the singing sword Balak |
| Phasaelus | Herod the Great's older brother |
| Rachel | Sigh's ewe sheep |
| Rachel | The wise woman who tutored Raz |
| Raz | Master of the Mysteries |
| Seh | Seth's ram sheep |
| Sepheth (Seph) | Master of Languages |
| Set | Clay and Dawn's third son |
| Sigh | Clay and Dawn's second son |
| Simeon | Prophesied at Jeshua's dedication |

| | |
|---|---|
| Uriel | The angel that replaced Halel over Delight, who will precede the Promised One |
| Zerah | The servant girl who introduced the King to Nebo, then served Nebo and his son |
| Zillah | Mishimar's black stallion Shadow |

# About the Author

Bill has always been a story teller. His wife says he still tends to share the truth creatively and with a flair for the dramatic. He grew up in south Seattle and has lived in Tacoma, Washington since 1972.

Initially working in hospitals (he completed half his RN education), Bill joined the Boeing Airplane Company in 1979. The last 15 years of his 32 year career he taught Employee and Leadership Development. Bill often developed and taught his own material and has written numerous short stories and dramas, culminating in his first published novel "Amidst the Stones of Fire" in 2017 and its sequel "Out of the Sanctuary" in 2018.

Now retired, he spends his time teaching, mentoring, acting in community theater, writing, and enjoying his family. Bill and his wife of more than fifty years, Nancy, live near their three children and seven grandchildren.

If you can't find Bill in his home-office, he is probably across the street playing with the neighbor's dog, Stacy.

# Advent Calendar

# December 1

**Begin saving for a special gift**

# December 2

**Bake cookies and
give them to your neighbors**

# December 3

**Do a random act of kindness
for a stranger**

# December 4

**Collect all of the household trash
and put it in the garbage**

# December 5

**Put away all of your stuff at night
before you go to bed**

# December 6

**Clean off the table and
do the dishes**

# December 7

**Smile at everyone you meet today**

# December 8

**Visit a Senior Center
(read to them, sing together, just listen)**

# December 9

**Write someone a Thank You Note**

# December 10

**Add someone new to your prayers**

# December 11

**Put a bottle of water and a snack in the car and share it with someone who is homeless**

# December 12

**Draw and color a picture for someone**

# December 13

**Fast one meal/week and give to a hunger relief organization**

# December 14

**Say "Please" and "Thank You"
more often**

# December 15

**Write someone a love letter or poem**

# December 16

**Feed the ducks**

# December 17

**Give someone a back rub**

# December 18

**Share a candy bar with a friend**

# December 19

**Take someone's animal for a walk**

# December 20

**Love someone who is not
usually very loveable**

# December 21

**Have a second dessert**

# December 22

**Learn to say "Merry Christmas"
in three other languages**

# December 23

**Walk around your neighborhood
and pick up any trash you see**

# December 24

**Tell someone what you appreciate
about them**

# December 25

**Buy the "special gift" you have been saving for and give it to the person you bought it for**

Made in the USA
Monee, IL
07 May 2021